The Ivy Creek Sewing Circle

The Ivy Creek Sewing Circle

Tammy Robinson Smith

THIS BOOK WAS PREVIOUSLY PUBLISHED AS EMMYBETH SPEAKS.

ISBN: 9781086476286

The Ivy Creek Sewing Circle

Cover Design by www.StunningBookCovers.com

This book is dedicated to all the mountain girls . . .

Help one another is part of the religion of our sisterhood.

~Louisa May Alcott

Present Day

My best friend, Karen, called early this morning to let me know Sissy Hudson died last night. Karen's younger sister is married to Mrs. Hudson's son, Tom. It breaks my heart to think that she was the last living member of The Ivy Creek Sewing Circle.

They are all gone now. It seems like just a minute ago they were sitting around our kitchen table sewing on lap quilts for the residents of the nursing home, eating cake, drinking coffee and chronicling the happy times and sad times that came their way.

Those women meant so much to me when I was growing up. I am not sure if they ever knew how much they influenced the decisions I made later in life. All I know is I would not be the woman I am today if it weren't for them teaching me about life, friendship, and the meaning of a good laugh, or a good cry.

Now, I understand how much they helped my family and me back in the summer of 1971. I am sure I didn't know anything about what it meant to be a strong woman back then, but, before another year passed, I had seen it in action.

Those women taught me that being a woman did not mean I ever had to take a backseat and let life happen to me. They taught me that women are strong enough to take care of themselves and their families no matter what obstacles they encounter.

I will be making a trip out to Ivy Creek in a few days to mourn the passing of the last original member of that special group of women. One thing is for sure, I will never forget what they taught me that summer . . . the summer I learned "Girl Power" wasn't just a catchphrase. It was a way I could live my life.

Chapter 1

I've got a favorite hiding place, and it's best to get into it early on Thursday mornings. That's when my momma's sewing circle comes over to our house and works on lap quilts for the old people that stay at Sunny Meadows nursing home out on Dogwood Road.

I've been there with my momma when she takes the quilts to give to Miss Gertrude; I think she's the lady in charge out there. She's big and fat and has gray curly hair and she smells like peanut butter. In case you ever see her. I sure would hate to be an old person like those people out there in that place. They smell bad, like when Timmy pees in his pants and don't tell Momma, cause he's too busy playing outside. Then he wonders why he itches all the time. He never washes his private parts even though he tells Momma he does. I know he don't, because he lies to her about most everything having to do with taking a bath or washing his hands. I hope he gets germs and dies. It'd serve him right.

Now me, I'm a different story. I'm nine-years old going on forty, according to my grandma. And I do like to know what's going on. That's why I'm here in my hiding place this morning. It's a trick getting in here on Thursday morning. First, I have to take my little brother Timmy down the road to Grandma and Grandpop's house for Momma. Then I have to sneak back up here and get in place. Grandpop and Timmy know I come back up to the house, but, I'm pretty sure they never give a thought as to what I'm doing. Momma and Grandma just figure I'm in my room reading or listening to the radio. Then, I wait until the kitchen is good and empty and hightail it into the corner cabinet. So far, so good. I've not been caught. I never do just out and out lie to anybody about where I go, but I don't exactly confess to nothing either.

The sewing circle is supposed to start at 10 o'clock, but wouldn't you know Miss Hawkins gets here early just to see what she can catch us in. That's what my grandma always says. She says Miss Hawkins don't have no life of her own, so she goes around butting in everybody else's. She lives up on Milk Holler Road. That's because that's where her daddy lived and made all his money. He had a big old dairy farm up there, and then he died and left all his money to Miss Hawkins. I guess she never did marry because no one never did ask her. If I's a man I wouldn't ask her. She is one hateful old biddy. She never does smile at us younguns, and always acts like we're in the way as soon as she walks in the room. Momma says it's not Christian, the way I'm all the time talking bad about people; but then she's always telling me to tell the truth so I can be a good Christian. Well, it's true Miss Hawkins is one hateful old biddy; but I reckon I'm not supposed to tell the truth about that if anyone asks me; but nobody ever does.

I have to stoop really low to get into my hidey hole here in the kitchen. I have to duck down and climb into the corner of the cabinet; then, I push all the cans of peas and corn out of the way so I can have a place to sit. I can't hold my head all the way upright; but if I lean over to the left against the wall, I can almost keep from getting a cramp in my neck. I have to leave the cabinet door a little bit open, and then I just pray to Jesus no one notices and closes it shut. It'd be just like Miss Hawkins to close the door if she saw me in here. Then Momma'd find me dead when she went to get a can of peas to heat up for supper tonight. I bet if she did Timmy would still want to eat supper before they took me to the funeral home. I think you can live for a couple of hours though in a closed-up place. I just try not to think about it because the truth is, I look forward to Thursday morning and hearing all the stuff my momma's circle talks about.

The hardest thing is trying to tell who is talking. I can recognize my momma's voice and my grandma's, and most of the time Miss Hawkins's voice, except when it gets soft. I just hate that too, because that's when I know I'm missing something really good, like maybe about making babies or somebody drinking. She always knows about stuff like that. Sometimes, after she leaves, I hear Momma tell Grandma that she wonders if Miss Hawkins just makes that stuff up, seeing as she don't have a life and all.

Then there's Mrs. Maiden. She's real pretty and awful sweet according to Grandma. I never did understand how you could be awful and sweet at the same time, but that's what Grandma says. She's real skinny and Miss Hawkins is all the time trying to get her to eat more; but Mrs. Maiden just always laughs real polite like, and tells her no, she doesn't need any more coffee cake, or whatever we have that day, just black coffee please. Momma says she thinks Mrs. Maiden's had a good upbringing because she's always using good manners. I know she's educated. I heard Mrs. Maiden tell my grandma that she graduated from Steed Business College over there in Johnson City where she's from, and that she worked in an office building downtown. She's knows typing and stuff. Grandma's all the time telling me to study good in school so I can go on and get more schooling. I'm all the time wondering why I would need to go on and get more schooling, if I done good in the school I was in. Sometimes it just don't make sense to me what grownups say.

"Lordy Mercy, Mama. What did you do? Make enough sticky buns for us and the Mormon Tabernacle choir? We'll never eat all of those this morning."

Momma's running around the kitchen now wiping down everything with a wet dishrag and shining it dry. She's afraid the other women will say she's not a good housekeeper. Who wants to be if you ask me? When I get old and live in the city, I'm gonna have me a housekeeper. I don't like to run around shining stuff. It all just gets dirty again.

Oh, I sure do hope Miss Hawkins don't eat her gut full of them sticky buns and take home the leftovers. That's one thing about being in my hidey hole when the ladies are here, I don't get the opportunity to eat until they've left. I just love Grandma's sticky buns. She makes the best ones—they're all soft and gooey and warm and it just makes my mouth water thinking about them. Maybe Grandma will put me some back on top of the refrigerator. Sometimes she does stuff like that for Timmy and me. Momma says she spoils us rotten. Timmy sure does smell like he's rotten most of the time.

"Just put on a pot of coffee, Darlene. Them women will be here before you know it. You know Myrtle Hawkins always gets here half an hour early. That's just the nosiest ole' so and so, Lordy sakes. She just don't seem to have no idey how to have a conversation without buttin' into your business someway or other. Jesus would have to love her because the devil couldn't stand to be around her for more'n ten minutes." That's my grandma. She says it like it is.

"Now, Mama, please don't be talking like that. Miss Hawkins can't help but be lonely way out there in the country, farther out than we are! Hardly anyone ever goes to visit her. You know she told us last week that no one had even been to her house since the youth group went out there caroling last Christmas Eve. Why, coming here on Thursday mornings is the biggest highlight of her week, next to going to church on Sunday."

Momma's all the time trying to be Christian-like in her heart and ways. She says me and Grandma ought to take lessons from her. I like me and Grandma just the way we are.

"Well, if you ask me, if you start out alone and grouchy, you wind up alone and grouchy."

"Mama! I declare you have the most vicious tongue sometime. You watch what you say. Why, even Emmybeth is starting to sound like you. Now you just hush up."

"Well, all's that I'm saying is most old people that wind up soured on the world and all alone, was that way when they was young. Now, you take Myrtle; I remember the time we all went on the Sunday School picnic when we was in the MYF. You know, back then before we were United Methodists with the Brethren and all, we was just plain ole' Methodist.

Anyways, we all went down to the little picnic shelter there below the church on the creek. The girls was getting the food and drinks all ready, and the boys was putting the stuff together to have to make ice cream later on—Lord, it was probably 90 degrees in the shade; it was the middle of July you know. Anyways, when us girls was puttin' the food out, old Myrtle went a runnin' to the youth leader and started telling him all about how us girls was gossipin' and takin' the Lord's name in vain, which by the way wasn't true; but you know how she is. Well, he comes over and starts to fussin' at us, and I popped up and said, 'Now, Mr. Evans, it was Tom Evans's oldest boy Paul, now, Mr. Evans' I said, 'You know Myrtle likes to stir up things. We're not a gossipin', and we're not a takin' the Lord's name in vain. However, Myrtle is a big, fat liar and that's the truth.'"

"Mama, I don't believe . . . well, actually I do believe you said that!"

Momma's laughing now. Grandma always gets her going. I don't believe Momma's quite as Christian in her thinking as she says she is. She's good and kind, but I'm telling you— Grandma's just plain funny when she gets on a roll; and she can even get Momma to laughing.

"Yes, I did. And you know ole' Myrtle did have the decency to at least blush a little bit, and of course then she got to sputterin' and coughin' and sayin' it was so. But then, Mabel Jean Hasser chimed in and told Mr. Evans we wasn't doin' nothin', it was just Myrtle tellin' tales. Of course, Mr. Evans just looked real mean at all us girls, and said to stop actin' like we was heathens. Anyway, what I'm tellin' you, is that Myrtle's always been Myrtle and always will be Myrtle.

She just knows she can make you feel sorry for her; and you'll send the leftover dessert home with her, rather than givin' it to your own children."

Way to go, Grandma. Keep those sticky buns here for me and old stinky britches.

"Oh, Mama! Sometimes, I just don't know what to do with you. You'd better be quiet now. Miss Hawkins's car is turning into the driveway."

The percolator is dripping now and the sticky buns are right by Miss Hawkins's chair. I'll never get a bite now. Probably won't be no leftovers the way she packs away the sweets. I can hear her car coming up the driveway. Daddy says it's an old piece of crap, and he can't believe it still runs. It's got them funny looking fins on the back, like the cars from my momma's high school yearbook. She graduated fourth in the class of 1959 from Ivy Creek High School. Daddy would have been in her class, but he dropped out in his junior year to start working in Papaw Jack's garage. That's his daddy. There was a real bad accident the summer before my daddy's junior year when one of the car's fell on Papaw Jack and squished his legs. He gets around with a cane, sorta. Mostly he just moves from one chair to the next and runs his mouth, according to Daddy. Daddy says he just sits and bosses him; but Daddy says it's no different than it's always been with Papaw Jack; it's just now he can't walk too good. I like Papaw Jack though. He's always got Starlight peppermints in his pocket for Timmy and me. They kinda smell like car grease. Of course, so does Papaw Jack. Granny May, his wife and my daddy's mother, is dead. She died before I was born, so it really doesn't hurt me to think about her, not to be disrespectful or anything.

"Darlene!"

Golly, Miss Hawkins sure hollers loud. "Darlene, are you here honey?"

Miss Hawkins can see Momma and Grandma through the back-porch door. I don't know why she acts like she can't.

"Yes, Miss Hawkins, come on in."

"Well, honey, I didn't know if you'd be up and ready or not. I'm a little bit early, but you know, my father always said you were just plumb lazy if you couldn't make the effort to get where you were going a little bit early. Lord, Esther, I didn't see you there. Why are you out so early this morning?"

"Well, Myrtle, I don't know why you'd be so surprised to see me hear. Darlene is my daughter, and we do meet here every Thursday morning. Don't take one of them rocket scientist to figure that one out."

"Miss Hawkins, why don't you come over here and sit down while I pour you a cup of coffee?"

I know Momma. She's trying to keep the peace. Grandma says she always has ever since she was a little girl.

"Now, Darlene, you don't need to go to any trouble. I never like to put people out on my account."

Grandma's snort is a little louder than I bet she meant to do it. Momma won't like that.

"You do have real cream don't you? I just hate that new powder stuff people's always trying to put in your coffee. I can stand to drink it with milk if y'all can't afford real cream, but now good sweet cream is what really makes your coffee. And I do like to drink mine out of real china. Do you have real china Darlene? Did you have a china pattern when you got married? I had one all picked out when I's a teenaged girl. Now, my mother said I was just mooney eyed, and I'm inclined to agree now, but it never hurts to be prepared."

I can't imagine why she would think she would need to be prepared for a wedding. Grandma says no man would marry a woman with more hair on her chin than he had on his head. Apparently, Miss Hawkins don't pluck her chin hairs to suit Grandma. I can see Momma heading back toward the table with the Miss Hawkins's coffee.

"Here you go, Miss Hawkins. Here's your coffee in a china cup, just like you like; and yes, as a matter of fact, I do have some real cream. I believe you mentioned last week that the powdered cream wasn't to your liking."

"Yeah, Myrtle, I believe you always have something to say about the service wherever you go."

Grandma's sounding kinda edgy now. Miss Hawkins better watch out. Grandpa always says you don't want to get Grandma riled up.

"Now, Esther, you know that's not true. I was just stating what I like. I don't reckon there's no law against having some preferences. Besides, we always used our fine china over home; that's just how I was brought up, I can't help that."

"Yeah, well . . ."

"Mama, can you go get those glass plates for me from the sideboard in the dining room?"

Grandma stomps out of the room.

"Well, I declare. No use to get huffy."

"Oh, Miss Hawkins, she's not huffy. Mama's just heavy footed."

Grandma sure would like to hear her say that. I can see Grandma's feet now coming back into the room. She's not stomping. Good thing for ole' Miss Hawkins.

"Here you go, honey. Want me to go ahead and fill up these plates with the buns?"

"Oh, don't worry, Esther, I can get my own."

What's the matter Miss Hairy Chin? Afraid you won't get your share if my grandma fills your plate. Oh no, there I go again. Momma would skin my hide if she could hear me thinking.

"I'm sure you can, Myrtle."

"Mama, there's Sissy Maiden. Come on out here with me to the porch and hold the door, so I can help her bring in those bags of batting and that scrap material the fabric store donated. Miss Hawkins, you just stay right there, and help yourself to those buns."

"Yeah, Myrtle, just stay right there. We wouldn't want you to have to get up."

"Humph," I hear Miss Hawkins grunt as soon as Momma and Grandma get out the door.

If I scoot down just so, I can look out the cabinet door and see what Miss Hawkins is doing. Oh, Lordy, Grandma's gonna have a fit. I can't believe that old biddy is running her fat finger around the edge of the plate with the sticky buns on it, getting the icing, and then licking it off. Oh gross, now she's going back around the other way. I'm gonna puke right here all over the peas and corn. Ain't no way I'm eating one of those buns now. Eeewee. I'm not gonna tell Timmy about this, well, that is until he's taking a bite of one of the leftover sticky buns. Now, there's no sense in that. Momma's all the time telling us to act like we weren't raised in a barn. Ole Miss Hawkins must've been raised in her daddy's milk barn, instead of in the house with the china cups like she claims.

"Come on in here, Sissy, and set this stuff down. Just put it here by the table. We're going to have a cup of coffee and a little bite to eat first. You too, Evelyn. I'm so glad you decided to come. It's so hard to get people who will sew with us. Miss Hawkins is here too. Look, Miss Hawkins, Sissy brought Evelyn Frazier with her today to help us quilt."

Momma's so good at making everybody feel comfortable when they come in the house. She says, according to Emily Post, it's the mark of a good hostess. Momma's all the time reading stuff like that and trying to make me learn it—for my own good. She says when I'm a grownup married woman, I'll be wanting to know how to be a good hostess, and a good housewife. Not me, no sirree. When I grow up, I'm gonna live in an apartment in the city, just like Mary Richards on the *Mary Tyler Moore* show. I just love it when she throws her hat up in the air when the show begins. That's gonna be me someday. I'll have a really cute apartment with shag carpet over every floor, even in the bathroom. I just love the way it feels on your feet. Karen Mullin's daddy put shag carpet in their new rec room. Her daddy's a carpenter, and he made a room in the basement where they have their television and two big old recliners. Karen and me just love to go down there, and sit in those seats, and eat popcorn and watch *Gilligan's Island* in the afternoon.

"Well, Sissy, I see you've brought us a guest. Evelyn, good to have you."

"Myrtle, Evelyn ain't no guest. Her people's been coming to Ivy Creek United Methodist Church longer than yourn'."

There goes Grandma again. I reckon Momma will have to separate her and Miss Hawkins like she does me and Timmy when we get to fussing.

"Evelyn, do you take sugar or cream in your coffee?" Momma is pouring coffee into the ladies' cups now.

"She's got the good cream, child, not that powdery stuff. Darlene, could you warm my coffee for me if it wouldn't be too much trouble?"

"Why sure, Miss Hawkins, as soon as I take care of Evelyn."

"Cream would be fine, Darlene; but, really, let me do it. You don't need to be waiting on me."

"No, no, just sit down there, and I'll get everybody's coffee cup filled up. We'll eat up these sticky buns and get to our quilting. Now, that's funny. Mama, did those children come back up here when we were outside helping Sissy and Evelyn? Sometimes they run in the front door when I'm out back. It looks like to me somebody's run their finger through the icing on the edge of this plate."

"Not that I know of, Darlene. I was helping you, remember? How about you, Myrtle? You was here in the house."

That's the way, Grandma. Bust her. Check her breath.

I guarantee it smells like icing from a sticky bun.

"Well, now, it seems to me, Darlene, that little girl of yours might have come running in and out of here while I was powdering my nose."

You old witch! Eeww, I hope you die more than I hope Timmy gets germs and dies. Of course, if he eats one of those sticky buns you've been licking on, maybe I'll get two birds with one stone.

"Emmybeth. Emmybeth!"

Oh, Lord Jesus, now I pray, Momma won't come looking for me.

"Oh, Darlene, just let that youngun' alone. Hard telling who's had their fingers on the plate this morning."

Lord Jesus, I thank you and I thank Grandma. And please forgive me for wishing that old witch dead. Amen.

"Oh, well. I guess it doesn't matter. We really do need to get started. We can just finish our coffee and sweets while Mama tells us what we need to do today. Okay then. Mama, why don't you tell us where we need to start and what we need to get finished today?"

"Okay, honey. Let's see. Now looks like accordin' to this list I got from the UMW, they've had two new residents move in out there at Sunny Meadows. We really need to get them two quilts done today so you can get out there with them, Darlene. And now let me see . . . Miss Gertrude wanted to know if we'd sew up some Christmas stockings for the people who work there, and of course all the residents, you know, to hang on the mantel in the sittin' room. She'd like to have them by the first of December, if we could finish them. She said just make them out of some red felt and big enough to put two or three candy canes in, and maybe some fruit and whatnot. Whaddyall' think girls? Could we do it?"

"Esther, I think that's just a fine idea. Miss Gertrude and them girls works real hard out there at that nursing home.

Why, you know some day, when I can't take care of the house and all, I think I'll just move out there with the rest of the old folks."

Yeah, and I bet that's the day the rest of them folks will decide to move out, Miss Witchy Poo Hawkins. You know she even looks like old Witchy Poo on *HR Puffin Stuff*. It comes on TV on Saturday mornings, and Timmy and me watch it every week. He gets scared sometimes, but they really ain't much to be scared of on there except old Witchy Poo.

"I think that's fine, Mama, if we get started on them right now. It's already almost the first of August, so we'd really only have a little more than three months to work on them, and keep up with the lap quilts. Of course, we'd really have to have them done before Thanksgiving, because we wouldn't be meeting those last two weeks in November with the holiday and all.

What about you girls, Sissy? Evelyn?"

"I don't know about Evelyn, but it's okay with me."

"Same here, Darlene. I'm new at this, so whatever y'all want to do, I'll just go along with it."

"All right, Mama. When I take these two quilts out there Saturday afternoon, I'll tell Miss Gertrude we'll do it."

"Okay, now, let's look here at what we got started last week. Darlene, did you bring that batting in here?"

"Yes, Mama. Remember we got it out of Sissy's car?"

"I declare. I can't remember nothin' no more. Yes, now let's just get it here spread out on the table."

I swear I'm getting a crick in my neck sitting in this cabinet. I'm still small for my age, so I fit in here almost as good as I did last year when I was going into the third grade.

I'll be in fourth grade at Ivy Creek Elementary School come September. I sure hope I'm in Mrs. Miller's class this year. She's all pretty and young and wears clothes like you see in the fashion section of Momma's *Redbook*—you know the part where they show pictures of the young career women. I see Momma looking at that, and I know she must want clothes like they have. She makes most of her clothes from Simplicity patterns, except one time, Daddy took her to what they call The Miracle Mall in Johnson City. She got a real nice black wool coat from Parks-Belk, and it only cost twenty-five dollars. It was marked down half of half, and Momma looked so pretty in it. It was her early Christmas present last year, and she wore it to the Christmas Eve service at church. Everybody was looking at her, and you could tell they was thinking how pretty she was. I could have busted I was so proud.

". . . and then I said to Hazel, I said, 'No, you can't be telling me the truth,' and she said, 'Yes, I am.'"

"Miss Hawkins, let's decide what kind of trim we're going to put on the stockings."

Oh, shoot. Momma'll try to hush up Miss Hawkins and I'll never hear what's going on.

"Well, now, Darlene, I think just some cotton balls glued on the top would be sufficient. Now, Hazel told me it is true that Edna and Bert Thompson's youngest daughter is expectin' a baby, and she just got married in June right after graduation. Now, let me tell you, that baby is due on Valentine's Day, and you can't tell me there's nothing fishy goin' on with that. Sounds like to me there was a little something going on with that girl before she got married. She always was trouble, feisty little thing she was. I told myself years ago she'd make trouble for her mama and daddy one day, and here she's gone and broke their hearts like this."

"Oh, Myrtle, that's just not true! I saw Edna down at the Giant supermarket last Friday and she was so excited about Patty's baby. If it's a little boy they're gonna name him Wayne; after Bert and Edna's oldest boy. You know the one that was killed in Vietnam a couple of years ago. And as far as when or how that little baby gets here, who cares but you and that old Hazel Griffin. She's got no need to talk as far as I'm concerned. You might ask her how her older sister got born six months after her mama got married."

"Now, Momma, Miss Hawkins, we really need to get on with this quilting if we're going to have start making Christmas stockings next week."

How do you reckon Mrs. Griffin's sister got born in six months? I remember when Momma had Timmy. I was just real little. It was the year before I started kindergarten, up the road at the Presbyterian church where they've got one; a kindergarten for five-year-olds that is. Anyway, Momma marked off nine months on the calendar, and every month we went out for ice cream, as it got closer to when Timmy was to get born. I know Momma got real fat from eating all that ice cream, but I didn't. It must take some women longer than others to get their babies born. I know there must be some other stuff that happens too. Like you have to be married according to Momma, and you have to let your husband hold you real close, according to my best friend Karen Mullins. Karen said she went in her momma and daddy's bedroom one night after she had a bad dream, and they was holding each other real close. That must have something to do with getting babies, because Karen's got three little sisters, and her momma's going to have another baby in November. I just can't believe you'd want to hold a man real close if it was just gonna make you have babies all the time like Karen's momma. She's really not as pretty as my Momma, and she always has baby spitup on her blouse. I'm just not going to let that happen to me. You never see baby spitup on Mary Richards clothes, and you ain't gonna see none on me.

"All I'm saying, Esther, is she is gonna have a baby; and it's just barely gonna be born on the right side of the sheets. T'ain't no surprise to me though. I coulda told you years ago."

"Uh, Darlene, now I'm new; and I don't want to be butting in; but don't you think we could do a little appliqué here on top of these quilts and make them a little more special? If you'll just reach me those scissors, I can cut out a flower, or even a cross and dove. My great Aunt Mabel Jean taught me how to make little patterns and cut them out, then you just stitch it on top like so . . ."

"Oh, Evelyn, that's so pretty. I think you're really going to be a big help to us. We were just talking last week about how we might need to try something different on these quilts, weren't we Sissy? Now, Sissy, you've been real quiet this morning. How are you getting along? Have you had any luck looking for a part-time job?"

"Well, Darlene, as a matter of fact I'm going to work next week. Just three days a week at Ed Hudson's insurance agency, mainly answering the telephone, and filing and typing reports. He really needs the help with his wife being sick . . ."

"How is Sue Ann getting along, Sissy? I baked a peach pie for them last week; but when I stopped by, Ed said she was in the bed. I reckon he must have been awful worried. I declare that boy didn't even ask me in, after I went to the trouble to bake that pie and deliver it. I kept trying to get in past the front door, but he just wouldn't have it."

"Did you ever think Sue Ann might have been restin' Myrtle?"

Yeah, Myrtle . . . I mean Miss Hawkins. I swear Grandma sounds like she's gonna cut loose on Big Mouth anytime now.

"Yes, I suppose, Esther; but he really could have let me come in and look at Sue Ann. They say the cancer's just about eat her up. It's just a matter of time, and there's poor Ed and that boy of theirs. What is his name? He's a little slow; isn't he, Darlene? Didn't you have him in Sunday School last year?"

"Yes, Miss Hawkins, I had Tommy in Sunday School; and he's a right fine little boy. Just a little shy. He'll grow out of it. Sissy, tell us about Kenneth. Is he still doing those long hauls for his uncle's trucking company?"

"He sure is, Darlene; and it seems like the long hauls are getting longer all the time. He was gone six days and nights last week to California, and he's back out on the road this week to Wisconsin. I'm hoping he'll get in Saturday evening, and at least be able to make it to the homecoming at church this Sunday."

"My, uh, my husband used to be gone like that too. He wasn't a trucker, but Larry used to work out of town on construction. It was real good money, but it just got to be so hard with him gone all the time . . . and then well, then after

Larry Junior and all . . . I just needed him at home here with me."

I bet Mrs. Frazier's got tears in her eyes now. She always does when she talks about Larry Junior. That was her little baby that died. Momma and Daddy and me went to the funeral home when they had visitation. Timmy was just a baby, and Momma and Daddy left him with Grandma, so as to not upset Mrs. Frazier and her husband. Momma tried to make me stay with Grandma and Grandpop, that night but I wouldn't. I wanted to see the little baby, even though I didn't tell Momma that, but I did. He looked like one of those angels in the Children's Picture Bible in the Sunday School classroom at church. Larry Junior's heart wasn't good, and he died in his sleep. Mrs. Frazier was just a cryin' and going on. Momma finally made Daddy take me outside, and we sat in the car and ate the Hershey kisses he's all the time giving me—even though Momma tells him he's gonna rot out my teeth. It was just so sad and I know it's probably wrong, but I really do like to see stuff like that . . . like when somebody's died or in the hospital. It's always just a little bit exciting if you ask me. At least I get to get all dressed up and go somewhere. Most of the time I'm just stuck here with ole' Timmy.

"Now, Evelyn, the best thing you could do is go ahead and have another baby. That's just the medicine for you. When Pauline Tilden miscarried them twins, why, she was expecting again three months later. Now she's got that one and another one on the way. You're young, Evelyn. You and Larry will have lots of younguns. Although, I never seen the use of having too many, just running around messing into everything."

"Excuse me, y'all, I just . . ."

Oh Lordy, Grandma's gonna kill Myrtle Hawkins for sure. Mrs. Frazier's done run out of the room, and with the way her head is bent down I bet she's a crying.

"Myrtle Hawkins without a doubt you are the most thoughtless old . . ."

"Mama!"

"Now Esther, don't you be startin' on me. That girl's just got weak nerves like her Granny Cumbow did. She's young. That baby wasn't more'n three months old when it died. She didn't have time to get too attached to it."

"Myrtle, you wouldn't know love if it hit you square up the side of the head."

Yeah, Grandma. Why don't you hit her up the side of the head? I'll come out of this cabinet to see that.

"Myrtle, you've never had a youngun' or anybody else for that matter. That girl carried that baby for nine months and poured her heart and soul into him for the three months he lived. He was her child. You don't get over that, and besides, one child can't replace another. Leave her be. She just needs more time, not some old biddy tellin' her to forget."

"Well, I never . . ."

"That's the problem Myrtle, you never . . ."

"Mama, Miss Hawkins, please!"

"Darlene, I'll just go check on Evelyn. Are we almost finished up here?"

Mrs. Maiden is getting up to go check on Mrs. Frazier.

"Yes, I think so—Mama?"

"Yeah, yeah I can get the rest of this stitching done. Now, where did my glasses go to? I can't seem to find them, Darlene."

"On top of your head, Mama."

"I'll finish this one, Darlene. You can see my stitches are a lot more even than the stitches over there on your mama's quilt."

"Yes, Miss Hawkins."

Oh, I'd love to see the look on Grandma's face now.

"Darlene, Evelyn and I are going to run on to the beauty shop. We've both got appointments for 11:30 this morning."

"Darlene, I'm so sorry, I didn't mean to go on like that."

"Now, Evelyn, you don't have to apologize for anything. We all know what you've been through and it's not something you can get over easily."

"Come here, child, and let me give you a hug."

Grandma's hugs are the best. She'll make Mrs. Frazier feel all better.

"Now, Evelyn, you come back next week. We'd love to have you."

Yeah, bet she'll really want to come back if you're here, Miss Hawkins.

Chapter 2

"You dirty dog liar. You quit telling Momma I'm not washin' behind my ears."

"Timmy, Momma sent me in here to check on you, because I'm the oldest. Now, you shut up, and do what I say, or I'll holler for Momma again!"

"Maammaa!! Come in here and make her leave me alone! She's got cooties."

"Do not. Shut up, Timmy! I mean it, just shut up and wash behind your nasty ears, or I'm tellin' Momma."

"Maammaa!!"

"Goodness sakes, Timmy, what's the matter in here? I could've heard you from clear across the road. Emmybeth, you're supposed to be checking on him. What's the matter?"

Momma stoops down next to the tub and looks straight at me, with that look that means business.

"Momma, he's not washing behind his ears. You told me to check and see if he was, because I'm the oldest. I'm in charge."

"Momma, make her shut up and leave me alone. Even when her ears are clean they stick out funny."

"Do not!"

"Do too!"

"Enough! Both of you be quiet. Emmybeth, go on in your room and get in bed, right now. Timmy, you finish up your bath. If y'all don't get in bed and go to sleep I declare it's going to be time for sunrise. I swear. I've still got to go back out to the kitchen and ice the cake for the homecoming tomorrow at church. You children just wear me out sometimes."

"I'm sorry, Momma. I was trying to do like you told me, but Timmy just won't cooperate."

There you go you little jerk. Bet you don't even know what cooperate means, but I do because it's on our report cards . . . cooperation . . . and I always get an S for Satisfactory. If Momma would turn her back I'd stick my tongue out at you.

"Momma, you tell Miss Know it All Britches I do too co-awper-nate, I mean rate . . . well whatever."

"Emmybeth, just go get in the bed. I'll be in to listen to your prayers in a minute."

Maybe old Timmy will slip under the water and drown . . . oh no, there I go again. It's a good thing I'm gonna be saying my prayers in a few minutes. I pray every night to Jesus that I can try harder to be a better soldier for the Lord. That's what our Sunday School teacher tells us to do. Tomorrow at Sunday School I'll be getting my gold braided Bible bookmark because I memorized all my Bible verses in Vacation Bible School this summer. Now come this fall I'll be moving up to the fourth grade room, in the Junior Department. I'll be so glad to be out of the baby section and away from Timmy.

Every Sunday he comes running into my classroom like a big old baby wanting me to take him upstairs to the bathroom. It is just so embarrassing, and Sammy Coleman always sniggers when Timmy comes in. Sammy's all the time sniggering about something. Karen says he's got a crush on me, but he'd better not or I'll bust his mouth. Sorry, Jesus.

"Emmybeth, come on now, kneel down here beside the bed and let me hear your prayers."

"Yes, Momma. Dear Lord, God bless Momma and Daddy . . . and I guess, Timmy . . ."

"Emily Beth Johnson."

Ooops, guess she didn't like that . . .

"Yes, Momma. God bless Momma and Daddy and Timmy and Grandma and Grandpop and Papaw Jack and Old Brutus.

In case you don't remember, he's Papaw Jack's St. Bernard. God bless the little children in the poor people countries even though I don't know them, but my Sunday School teacher, Mrs. O'dell says they're hungry because their daddies won't work and their mommas just keep having younguns' . . ."

"Emmybeth!"

"Momma, that's what Mrs. O'dell says, I swear, you can ask Karen, she said it."

"Emmybeth, just finish your prayers. I need to finish that cake and put the ham in the refrigerator so it won't spoil before morning."

"Okay, okay. God bless Preacher Cates and Mrs. Cates and God bless Karen Mullins my best friend and . . . oh yeah, help me to be a better soldier for the Lord. Amen."

"Goodnight Emmybeth. Give me a kiss. I love you all the way around the world and back again sweetheart."

"Goodnight, Momma. I love you too."

I just love the way Momma always touches my cheek after she kisses me goodnight. I know she loves me good, and Daddy does too. He just hardly ever gets home in time to tuck me and Timmy in. He works late on Saturday nights at Papaw Jack's garage, at least that's what he says. Grandma says it's cause old Junior McCall comes by and keeps a jawin' to all hours. His daddy used to work for Papaw Jack when Daddy was a little boy. Daddy says Junior's a good mechanic, just kindly lazy. He works for Daddy sometimes, when Daddy can get him to. He never had no wife or kids, and lived with his mama and daddy even after he was all grown up. Now his daddy is dead, and his mother, who's the oldest resident out at Sunny Meadows, is almost one hundred years old. Her birthday is coming up the day after Thanksgiving according to Miss Gertrude. She was tellin' Momma all about it when we took the lap quilts out this afternoon. They're gonna have a big old party for Mrs. McCall "if she makes it," according to Miss Gertrude. It didn't look like to me that Mrs. McCall could make anything though. I could see her sitting in what they call the day room, where there's a color TV and a big old piano in the corner. Mrs. McCall was sitting in there in her wheelchair with her eyes closed. She was wearing a faded pink housecoat and white socks that didn't look like they fit her too good. She already looks dead if you ask me . . . but, I guess she'll enjoy having a birthday party . . . if she makes it . . .

"Emmybeth, Emmybeth it's time to get up. Your breakfast is ready. We need to get a move on, Emmybeth. You know you have to get all gussied up for church."

"Daddy, just five more minutes."

"Come on, punkin'. How's my pretty girl this morning?"

"Oh, Daddy, please don't turn on that light. It hurts my eyes."

"Come on, Emmy, rise and shine."

"Okay, Daddy, I'm comin'."

Oh, I just hate getting up of the morning. Grandma says I'll be late for the end of time, if the angel Gabriel blows his trumpet before seven o'clock in the morning. I don't care. I don't understand what the end of time is anyway, even if Preacher Cates is all the time preaching about it and saying we need to repent our sins. Grandpop don't like Preacher Cates when he starts to going on with all that stuff. He says Preacher Cates is starting to sound like a jack-leg preacher, and he wishes the District Superintendent would come in and catch him goin' on like a fool one Sunday morning.

Today's the homecoming at church. It's always fun for us children, well, that is after all the preachin' and singin', and talking about the ones that have gone on to be with the Lord, and the ones that have come from the furtherest away. It's always the same family that gets recognized for that every year. My Uncle Earl, Momma's brother from Knoxville, always comes and brings his wife, my Aunt Flora, and their daughter, who's my cousin Katherine. We can't call her Kathy, though, because Aunt Flora says that her formal name is Katherine, and that's what we should call her, please. Actually, me and Karen call her Old Booger Nose, when nobody's around, because of that one time she sneezed right big, and a booger flew out of her nose right across the table and landed on the shoulder of Miss Hawkins's dress. It was so funny. Aunt Flora took out a white lace handkerchief and started trying to clean up the mess, and then, of course, Old Booger Nose started crying because Karen and me was laughing so hard.

"Emmybeth, come on into the kitchen and start eating your pancakes. You're running out of time, and don't forget to put your housecoat over your dress. I'll braid your hair after you eat."

Momma always makes me put my housecoat over my Sunday clothes when I eat breakfast, so I don't spill nothing on them.

"Lord, Vernon, please turn down that gospel singing and don't try to hit the baritone notes. You'll never find them! You're getting as bad as your daddy keeping the sound up so loud."

"Now, Darlene, I'm just making a joyful noise unto the Lord. It is Sunday morning after all."

"Come here, Emmybeth, and give your daddy some sugar."

"Yeah, Emmybeth, give me some suurrgar. Kiss, kiss."

"Stop it, Timmy."

"Don't you kids start this morning. Emmybeth, you want maple syrup on your pancakes or Karo?"

"Just Karo, Momma, and lots of butter please."

"Okay, coming up. What about you Timmy? Are you finished and ready to get dressed?"

Momma doesn't even let Nasty Boy start getting dressed 'til he finishes eating. Timmy is one messy sight; looks like they would just take the garden hose to him, like we do to Old Brutus.

"Yes, Momma. Do I have to wear my suit? Why can't I wear my blue jeans and tenny shoes like Glenn does? His mom lets him."

"That's because they don't have no money for a suit you big stupid!"

"Emmybeth, stop that. If you two start again, you're going to spend all afternoon in your rooms after church. And Emmybeth, I've told you before not to talk about the Roberts family. They do the best they can."

Timmy's best friend is Glenn Roberts. He's actually an okay kid, even better than Timmy, except that he lisps, and everytime he says an S word he spits on you. His family lives up on Bingham Road. The houses up there are kinda small, and some of them have junk cars sittin' out in front, and old living room chairs on the porch. They're not like our three bedroom brick ranch house. Momma says it makes no difference and that Glenn is a sweet child and I'd better be nice to him. I just said they were poor, which is the truth. Momma's just plain funny about stuff sometimes. Not like Grandma.

"Come on, Timmy boy. Daddy'll help you get dressed up in your suit and tie. You and me will be the two best lookin' men in the church this morning."

"Ride me piggy-back Daddy!"

"Okay, hop on."

"Get out of here you two. Vernon you're just a bigger version of Timmy. You're my big boy and Timmy's my little boy."

"Yes sirree! You ready ranger?"

"Ready, Daddy!"

"Emmybeth, let me see, which dress do you want to put on today? Your pink sundress, or the light blue one with the sash?"

"Oh, Momma, the pink one. You know I don't wear that ugly old blue hand-me-down dress from Katherine."

"Now, Emmy."

"Momma, she always makes fun of me wearing her handme-down dresses. She says it's because Daddy don't make as much money as Uncle Earl. She says that's why I have to wear her worn out clothes."

"Emmybeth, there not worn out—she just outgrows them. Finish up, and I'll braid your hair after I get mine fixed. I just need to tease it up a bit and put on my dress."

"Okay, Momma. I'm almost done."

I can't wait to see Karen today. We always have so much fun together. Now, Katherine, I could never see again, and it would be all right—even if she is my cousin. She is so bossy, and such a blabbermouth. If Karen and me even look at her cross-eyed she runs and tells her mama.

"Come on in here, and sit at my dresser baby girl. I'll braid your hair and then you can take off your robe and put it back in your bedroom."

"Okay, Momma."

I just love sitting at Momma's dresser when she does my hair. It's almost like being at Char-Lita's beauty shop, where Momma goes and gets her hair fixed every Friday morning at 9 o'clock. Daddy teases her about never missing her hair appointment. She says it's her one luxury for taking care of him and us kids so good.

"Let's see, Emmybeth. If you're going to wear that pink sundress, let's do a ponytail braid with a pink ribbon at the bottom."

"Yes, Momma."

"Now, hold still, and don't be so fidgety."

"I'll try."

Every week we go through this. I try to hold still, but I swear, sometimes it really hurts my head when Momma gets to pulling so hard.

"Okay, if you'll just hold still a minute, Emmybeth, I've almost got this done. There you go sweetie pie. Run along and tell your Daddy and Timmy we're almost ready."

"Oh, How I love Je-sus . . . Oh, How I Love Je-su-us . . . Oh, How I Love Je-sus, be-ca-ause He first Loved me . . ."

"Emmybeth! Either you and Karen stop that snickering this instant or I'll send Karen back to sit with her mama and daddy."

"Sorry, Momma."

Karen's raisin' her eyebrows one more time, but I guess I'd better settle down, because I can tell when Momma means business! Karen and me just get so tickled watching Miss Hawkins in the choir when she's singing. She gets this real holy look on her face and lifts her eyebrows when she's trying to hit the high notes. Oh, Lordy, I hope my stomach don't start growling. Seems like Preacher Cates knows when the kids are starting to fidget and want to get out of the worship service. That's when he goes on extra long, and calls on the choir for two more verses during the altar call. At least we've already done all of the stuff for homecoming—you know the ones who've died, and the one's who've come from the most far away to be here. Of course it was Uncle Earl, Aunt Flora and Katherine again.

At least we didn't have to sit with them. Daddy ushered us into the pew across from them this morning. If you ask me, I don't think he likes Uncle Earl too good. Daddy practically pushed us into this pew when he saw Uncle Earl and Aunt Flora in the one across from the aisle. Aunt Flora has on her "city duds," that's what Grandpop calls them. He says she just thinks she's fancy being able to shop at all them stores down in Knoxville. Momma tells him to hush, but Grandma actually giggles when he says it, just like a girl. I can't wait to get out of here, but I do dread having to put up with Katherine this afternoon. She always leeches onto Karen and me, even though we don't like her. But Momma says I should be nice to her, seeing as she is my cousin, after all.

"Emily Beth, where do you think you're going? Daddy, Emily Beth and Karen are trying to run off and leave me."

"Why, honey, now I'm sure that's not so, is it Vernon? These girls can't wait to get with you, and hear all about what's going on down in the city these days — can they Vernon?"

"Emmy, you and Karen come on over here, and mind your manners, now. Sit down here with Katherine."

"Yes, Daddy."

"Yes sir, Mr. Johnson."

I hope Daddy doesn't see the way Karen's rolling her eyes now. She does that a lot when Katherine is around.

"Go, Katherine, sit there next to Emmybeth. You girls got you some fine lunch there to eat. Katherine just eats like a bird, don't you honey? Wants to keep her figure so the boys will chase after her, except her daddy's not gonna let them, is he honey?"

"Oh, Daddy."

Oh, Daddy, oh brother! What boy would want to chase after Old Booger Nose? What with things blowing out of her nose, and that chicken neck, and whiney voice.

"Vern, how's it going down at the garage? You still running it for your daddy?"

"Well, no, Earl, haven't you heard? The garage is mine, has been since 1960 when I bought it from my daddy. Didn't realize we hadn't let you know."

"Oh, yeah, uh, you know, that's what I meant . . . how is Jack doing these days?"

"Doing well."

There goes Uncle Earl again. Daddy just hates that, I always hear him talking to Momma after Uncle Earl leaves. Uncle Earl always acts like that Daddy is just running the garage for Papaw Jack, and that he don't own it; even though he knows that Daddy does to own it. Daddy's real proud that he bought the business from Papaw Jack. Says it's what men do, that they don't go sponging off nobody, not even their daddies.

"Sold any cars for your boss lately, Earl?"

"Yeah, yeah, sure enough, Vernon. Why, you just can't believe how business booms down in Knoxville, all the time some bigshot needing a new Cadillac for hisself or some little sporty thing for the wife. You know."

"I know."

"Oh, and Mr. Taylor, he's good to his chosen few, you know, like well, yours truly here. Top salesman now six months running. We got benefits too, you know. Why we even have dental, in case Katherine needs braces. Can't beat that, you know."

"I know."

Daddy always makes fun of Uncle Earl after he leaves— goes around saying "you know" after every sentence for days. Momma sure does get aggravated at him, but she slips up and laughs at him sometimes. It beats me how Uncle Earl could actually be Momma's brother. He's sure don't act like Momma. Momma's got two older sisters too, they're twins. One of them is named Claudetta, after Grandpop, and the other one is Etta Jean. They don't live near us, though. They married two brothers and moved up north, so their husbands could work in a factory in Indiana. We hardly ever see them; but Grandma and Grandpop always go up to visit every year.

"If you want, I could talk to Mr. Taylor, you know, put in a good word for you. Now, you'd probably have to work in the service department, you know, not out front in sales, but I'm sure he could find a place for you, you know. Why, you could move my sister and those younguns' down to the city, you know, be good for them. Why, I bet Flora could even get Darlene in the Jaycettes. She's president-elect this year. It's good for my customer base, you know. The more people, who know me, come to see me when they need a car."

"Yeah, well, Earl, just one problem with that plan, who'd run my business here?"

"Well, you know, just a thought, you know."

"Yeah, I know."

Daddy grins and looks over at me and winks. I know what he's thinking.

"Knoxville's a good place Vernon, got schools, and a big old mall and UT football."

"Really, Earl, you know we got schools here too. Why, Emmybeth'll be in the fourth grade this year over at Ivy Creek Elementary. Timmy will be starting first grade there after kindergarten. Then, of course, we've got the high school and good old East Tennessee State University over in Johnson City after that."

"Well, that's true enough, and you know, I did a year over there at East Tennessee State after high school. I think that's why Mr. Taylor relies on me, you know, me being a college man and all."

Oh, brother. Here comes Aunt Flora.

"Earl, there you are. Oh, hello, Vernon, Emily Beth, and now who's your little friend? You're that Mullins child aren't you?"

"Yes, m'am."

"Katherine, you need to get out of this hot sun. Well, I declare you're going to get burned to a crisp. Where's your shawl? You girls go over there, and get under that shade tree where Darlene and I are sitting. I'm going over here and speak to Preacher Cates and his darling little wife. I want to properly thank her for those peach preserves she gave us for coming from the longest distance away today. Katherine, your skin is so delicate; you'll just be a mess if you don't get in the shade."

"Yes, Mother. Come on Emily Beth, you too, Karen, I guess."

Oh shoot, here we go—with Miss Katherine Pain in the Patootie, bossin' us around. Man, and she looks so stupid today. I can't believe Aunt Flora makes her wear those shawls. It's a hundred degrees out here, but Aunt Flora's all the time worrying about Katherine catching a cold, or taking a chill, or some weirdo illness. If you ask me, who would really care if she got sick, other than Aunt Flora?

"Emily Beth, my mother said even if everyone else calls you by your nickname, I should call you by your formal name, Emily Beth."

What about I call you by your real name, Booger Nose? Guess I'd better not say that out loud.

"Whatever."

"Katherine, you know Emmybeth doesn't go by her full name."

"Karen Mullins, my mother says we should behave like civilized human beings, even if we're up here in the hills."

Old Katherine's probably still a bit mad at Karen and me over that whole Booger Nose incident. Like we could help laughing when she blew a booger on Miss Hawkins. It was funny!

"Come on. Mother says we should go over and sit in the shade, so I won't burn my delicate skin."

"Oh, all right, come on Karen, let's go over here. Daddy, we're gonna go over there under the maple tree. Okay?"

"Sure, honey, now you all be good."

"Okay, Daddy. Come on Katherine let's go."

"Just a minute, Emily Beth. I have to get my plate and drink."

Oh great, I get to watch her eat. Funny thing to me, she tries to be so proper, but when she chews her food, she keeps her mouth open. It's almost as disgusting as watching Miss Hawkins lick her fingers, when she was eating Grandma's sticky buns during the sewing circle meeting. What in the world did I do to deserve a cousin like Katherine? I bet that's what Miss Hawkins's cousins thought when they were kids.

"Emmybeth, I really need to run over and ask my mom something."

"No, you don't, Karen."

"Yes, I do."

"Oh, Emily Beth, just let her go."

That stinking Karen! She's rolling her eyes again. She's deserting me with Katherine. Karen, you're gonna pay for this later. Watch her laugh. Karen Mullins you'll pay for this even if you are my best friend!

"Emily Beth, let's sit here in these chairs. Mother said I shouldn't sit on the ground because it might be damp."

It's a funny thing to me that Aunt Flora even lets Katherine be outside. It's like she's afraid if Katherine does anything at all that she'll get sick and die. Big deal. Uh, oh. Sorry, Jesus. And there sits Momma, hope she's can't read my mind right now.

"Hello, Katherine. Emmybeth. Are you girls getting enough to eat? Timmy, say hello to your cousin Katherine."

"Hello, Katherine."

"Hi there, Timmy."

"Are you having fun here today Katherine?"

"Not really, Aunt Darlene. You know usually on Sunday afternoon, Mother and I go to the mall and shop. This is, well, you know, not so much fun."

"Oh, I'm sure there's lots for you girls to do after you finish your lunch. Right, Emmybeth?"

"Sure."

"Emmybeth?"

"Yes, Momma. We'll find something to do as soon as we've finished eating."

Shoot! Now I have to entertain Katherine all afternoon.

Darn that Karen's hide for deserting me like this. It's not that I don't like Katherine, it's that I HATE her! Even though Momma, and sometimes, even Grandma tells me that she's my only girl cousin, and we could be like sisters, if I'd just try harder. I still just don't like her. She has to wear her old stupid shawls, and she can't sit on the ground. I bet she's never even swung on a grapevine. Hey, there's an idea. Me and ole' Katherine will go swing on the grapevine swings, in the woods, down by the creek. If Momma's gonna make me entertain her, then I'll just make sure we do something I want to do!

"That's a cute dress Katherine. You certainly look all grownup today; but aren't you getting a little warm in your shawl? You can just take it off, and I'll hang it here on the back of my chair, if you like?"

"Oh, no, Aunt Darlene. Mother says I might catch a chill. Do you like my dress? Mother bought it for me in the Junior Miss department at Miller's, in the mall in Knoxville. I'm sure Emily Beth will be the only girl in school with one like it when she gets my hand-me-downs next year. Of course, it will probably be out of style, but only down in Knoxville, not here."

"You know Katherine, I'm not . . ."

"Emmybeth, are you finished with your lunch?"

"But, Momma, I . . . "

"Emmybeth, if you girls are finished why don't you find something fun for you and your cousin to do? Emmybeth, do you hear me? Now run on, and you watch out for Katherine. Timmy, slow down, and remember to chew with your mouth closed!" Geez, why didn't she tell that one to Katherine?

"Come on Emily Beth, but just make sure we're not out in the hot sun like my Mother said."

"Oh, all right."

Man, I hate it when Momma does that! She can always tell what's going to come out of my mouth before it gets there. I don't want Katherine's old hand-me-downs. I'd rather go to school naked. And, she's all the time acting like we live in the sticks, and she's so hot because she's from the city. Maybe it's time for Katherine to learn what it's like out here in the sticks.

"Slow down, Emily Beth."

"You hurry up. It's not that far. I want to show you where we play, and this is certainly in the shade. See all the trees."

"Well, I hope it's not too far into the woods. Mother said I shouldn't get this dress dirty. It's practically brand new."

"This is gonna be fun. We come up here to swing."

"I can't believe there's a swingset back here, Emmybeth. You better not be lying or I'll tell my mother . . . and yours too! Aunt Darlene said you were to watch out for me."

You know, sometimes I just can't help myself. I know I'm gonna get in trouble. I can almost smell it, but I just can't help myself. Sorry, Jesus.

Sorry Momma. I know she'll be the one I get in trouble with!

"Come on up here, Katherine, and we'll swing. You know, country style."

"What do you mean Emily Beth? You know I'm not supposed to get dirty."

Yeah, or cold, or hot, or burned in the sun, or anything else for that matter.

"Just come on, Katherine. Gee whiz. Don't you want to have fun? Do they do that where you live?"

"Yes, but where I live we are civilized. Why, we even have girl-boy parties, and we get dressed up to go to them."

Just like Jan Brady on *The Brady Bunch* I bet.

"I bet you've never even been kissed, much less played Spin the Bottle, or Post Office, Emily Beth."

"Yeah, cause I wouldn't want to Katherine. Here, let me show you our swing."

"There's no swing here, just a bunch of old vines. You tricked me Emily Beth Johnson."

"No, I didn't. I told you, this is how we swing. See, just catch hold here, and pull yourself up a little bit. See, it's easy. Oh yeah, first you better pull on the vine real hard, to see if it'll hold you. Then, just grab hold of it, and run with it a little bit, and pull yourself up in the air, and off you go! See, let me show you."

"Emily Beth, Mother would not like me doing this."

"Katherine, do you always do what your mother tells you? Bet she didn't tell you to play Spin the Bottle did she?"

"Well, no . . . and you better not tell her I did Emily Beth."

"Then you might just want to try swinging on this grapevine."

"You wouldn't dare tell her."

"Won't say I won't, won't say I will."

"Emily Beth, I hate you."

"I hate you too. Now, let's swing on some grapevines, Miss Kissy Lips!"

"Well . . . I might try . . . just once. But, if you don't catch me if I start to fall . . . I'll . . ."

"You'll what Kissy Face? Kiss. Kiss."

"Oh . . .Emily Beth I can't do this."

"Quit being such a big old baby and hand me that stupid shawl."

"It's not stupid."

"Yeah, right, and it's not a 100 degrees today either."

"Oh, all right. Here goes nothing."

"That's right, grab it real hard and tug on it . . . give it a run . . . and go! That's the way. Katherine . . . Katherine, you'd better open your eyes, and don't let go, or you're gonna . . ."

"AWWRRGGHHH!!!!!!!"

"fall in the . . . creek." Splash!!

Oh shoot, I can't believe she let go. Aunt Flora's gonna be so upset. Okay, Emmybeth, don't laugh.

"EMMIILLY BETH! I, I, I'm all wet and it's all your fault! You did this on purpose."

"Katherine, you're not supposed to LET GO OF THE VINE. Here, take your shawl and put it on. Aunt Flora'll never be able to tell. See, I told you it's fun. You gotta admit, you had fun."

"I'm going to go find Aunt Darlene, and I'm telling what you did!"

"And I'll tell Aunt Flora AND Uncle Earl you've been kissing boys down there in Knoxville, at your girl and boy parties." There. Gotcha. Whatcha gonna do now Kissy Face?

"MAMA . . .AUNT DARLENE!"

Oh shoot! Guess I underestimated ole Katherine. It's gonna be heck to pay now. "I can't wait to get out of these woods and go back home.

Back to civilization in Knoxville, Tennessee."

Yeah, me too, Katherine. I hope you go home real soon.

Chapter 3

Today's sewing circle ought to be real good, seeing as we had the homecoming service at church on Sunday. Seems like that always gives Miss Hawkins some real juicy stuff to talk about. Come to think of it, she may be talking about me and Katherine, and the stir we caused, when she came running out of the woods. Thank goodness I got through that afternoon without getting skinned alive. Seems that Uncle Earl used to swing on those same grapevines, when he and Momma was kids. He wasn't really mad, but Aunt Flora was; and she kept sayin' I was trying to kill Katherine. She gets real dramatic on occasion. And of course, Katherine acted like she was gonna die. Lord knows, I couldn't get that lucky. Sorry, Jesus. Grandma, and even Momma, took up for me, and said I was just trying to show her how to swing on the grapevines. They got some dry clothes for Katherine from the house so she could change. Aunt Flora made Uncle Earl get the Cadillac and head back home right then. Good riddance if you ask me! Maybe ole Katherine's wearing my hand-me-downs this week. She deserves that.

"Momma, I'm gonna run down to Grandma's with Timmy. Okay?"

"It's awful early, Emmybeth. My sewing circle won't be here for another hour."

Yeah, I know. I want to get my spot good and early. It's a good thing Momma can't hear what I think, or I'd always be in trouble!

"I know, but Timmy wants to go now."

"No, I don't, Emmybeth."

"Yes, you do, Timmy."

"Oh, you children, just go on before you start fussing. Timmy, you be a good boy for Grandpop while Grandma comes up here to sew. Emmybeth, you be good too. Don't you be fussing, and fighting, and making a lot of noise around Grandpop. He likes to watch his game shows of the morning."

"Yeah, and he likes to eat Little Debbies, too. We like the oatmeal cakes the bestest."

"Well, just make sure you don't eat too many, Timmy boy."

"Sure, Momma."

Yeah, right. I think he ate four last week. Grandpop said he thought Timmy was going to bust. I was kinda hoping he would!

"Come on, Timmy. Let's go."

I like it that Grandma and Grandpop live so close to us. We just have to walk out to the end of our driveway, and then through an empty field, and their house is just right there. Grandpop owns all of this land, well, except the lot Momma and Daddy bought from him, and built our house on. All of this used to be farmland when Grandpop was a boy. After my Grandpop got out of the Army, he stopped farming and opened the grocery store in Ivy Creek. He was the storekeeper at Creekside Grocery for a long, long time. Grandma worked there sometimes, too. Grandpop retired a couple of years ago though; so, now he just stays at home, driving Grandma crazy, according to the way she tells it.

"Emmybeth, do chickens give milk?"

"What?"

"I said, Emmybeth, do chickens give milk? They live on farms like cows."

"No, Timmy. Chickens don't give milk! Where'd you hear that? From Glenn Roberts?"

"No, I's just thinking."

"Well, don't hurt yourself."

"Huh?"

"Never mind."

Little brothers. Sometimes I could just squish his guts out. But I guess most of the time he's okay. As little brothers go.

"Emmybeth."

"Timmy, when it's just the two of us, you don't have to say my name every time you want to talk to me. Nobody else is here."

"Huh?"

"Never mind, what do you want?"

"Emmybeth." Oh brother.

"Yes, Timmy."

"Can Momma have puppies?"

"Timmy, I swear you are so dumb."

"Am not."

"Are too. Women don't have no puppies."

"Well, I was just wondering. Wouldn't you like to have a puppy? I would. Glenn's got nine puppies at his house. He said the mama had 'em, so I thought maybe our Momma could have some."

"He's talking about the mama dog, you do-do."

"Don't call me do-do. You stupid head."

"Well, at least I know women can't have puppies." I declare. He can be so silly sometimes.

"Grandpop, Grandpop. Here I am."

"Geez, Timmy. He can see you comin'. He's standing right there on the screen porch."

"There's my little buddy. How are you this morning? Come on in here to the kitchen. Emmybeth, get you a Little Debbie there on the table, if you want one. Timmy, are you ready to watch *Let's Make a Deal?*"

"You bet, Grandpop."

Sometimes I think Grandpop may like Timmy better than me. They're all the time watching his shows together and stuff. But you know, I like Grandma best and I think she likes me best. So it all evens out in the end.

"Emmybeth, you goin' back up to your house or stayin' here? If you're going, take you one of them cakes, honey, so you'll have a snack."

"Thank you, Grandpop."

"You're mighty welcome, young lady."

"Emmybeth, there you are."

"Hi, Grandma."

"Hi my sweet girl. I sure appreciate you helping me carry these pecan tassies and my sewing things up to the house."

"It's okay Grandma. I don't mind to help you."

"Now, Claude, don't you worry, I'll be back before lunch and get you fed! We know you don't want to be missin' any meals. Ain't that right, Emmybeth?"

Grandma laughs, but I don't think Grandpop hears her. He's already headed out to the living room to watch his shows with Timmy. Sometimes, I wonder if he does hear Grandma saying the stuff she does about him, and just acts like he doesn't. They sure are funny, my Grandma and Grandpop.

"Okay, sweetie. Let's see, get my sewing basket and we'll head on over. How's my girl this mornin'?"

"I'm fine, Grandma."

"I'm glad you're good. Lord knows after I spend the morning with Myrtle Hawkins I won't be!"

Grandma laughs at her own joke as we make our way back across the field to our house. The grass here in the field always itches my legs when Grandpop lets it get too high. Grandpop fusses about it growing so fast this time of year and getting so high, but Grandma says it doesn't seem to motivate him to get out here and keep it cut down where it oughta be.

"Well, Emmybeth, did you recover from your shenanigans with Miss Katherine Sunday afternoon?"

"I guess so, Grandma. It wasn't my fault. I tried to tell her not to turn loose of the vine, but, well, I guess I was too late and by then she was in the creek . . . but I don't think it hurt her as bad as she let on."

"Probably not. I know you and Katherine are not a lot alike. Maybe when she grows up and gets away from that dadblasted Flora . . . um, well, uh, now don't you go tellin' your Momma I said that. You know she don't like me talkin' about other folks in front of you. But maybe when Katherine grows up, y'all can be friends, as well as cousins."

"Maybe. I don't know. Hey, Grandma, want me to tell you a secret? Katherine told me not to tell her parents, but she didn't say a thing about not telling you."

"Well, what is it then?"

"Katherine said that down there in Knoxville, they have girl-boy parties, and guess what? She kisses boys at them parties she goes to! Isn't that just yucky, Grandma?"

"Emmybeth, I declare. You are just so funny sometimes. You know, one day before long, you might not think it's so awful to kiss a boy. Might even want a smooch from Sammy Coleman one day!"

"Eeeww, Grandma. That's nasty!"

Me and Grandma laugh as we're heading in the backporch door. I wouldn't sass Grandma for nothing in the world, but she just don't know what she's talkin' about. Me kissin' Sammy Coleman ain't never gonna happen. I know better than that!

Well, I dodged Momma and Grandma getting in my hiding spot and not a minute too soon. I can hear Miss Hawkins's car coming up the driveway. Seems like to me she comes earlier and earlier every Thursday morning.

"Mama, is that Miss Hawkins already? I swear. Here, take this rag and finish wiping off the kitchen sink. I'll go see if she needs help with anything getting out of the car."

"All right now don't be fussin' over the house. Everything's always shiny here, Darlene. I don't know why you worry so much. You sure don't get that from me!"

"Well, Mama, you're the one who taught me to shine! Seems like to me it was always my job at home to dust and shine! You're memory's not too good these days."

"Oh, just go see what Myrtle's a needin', I'm sure she needs something!"

"Mama, hush! Good morning, Miss Hawkins. Come on in here. Do I need to help you with anything?"

"I'm okay Darlene. Here, child, all I've got is my sewing basket with my quilting things in it. I can make it. Mornin', Esther. How you doin'? How's Claude these days? I didn't get to do much more than say hidee-do to him on Sunday, and he went off with Timmy. The youngun' was yankin' on him to go to the dessert table. You might want to keep an eye on him, Darlene. Don't want that child to go gettin' tubby."

I think I might just laugh out loud at that. Grandpop says he ain't never seen such a wide load as is on Miss Hawkins's hind end. Grandma always asked him what's he doing lookin' at Miss Hawkins's hind end, and Grandpop says who in the world could miss it?!

"Yes, Miss Hawkins. Would you like a pecan tassie with your coffee this morning?"

"Don't mind if I do. Just cream in my coffee, well maybe just a little sugar you know, to flavor it."

"Yes, Miss Hawkins."

"Well, Esther, I reckon you was glad to see Earl and Flora up here on Sunday. He must be a' doing well down there in Knoxville, driving a new, big shiny car, I seen. And that little Katherine, now there's a good youngun' if you ask me. Always minding her manners, and saying 'yes m'am,' and 'thank you,' like she should. It was such a shame that Emmybeth pushed her in the water and got her pretty little dress all wet. Why, with Katherine's fragile condition, she could have caught a cold or worse!"

You old biddy! If I was gonna push someone in the creek it'd be you. Except you'd probably splash all the water out and dry up the creek!

"Oh, now, Myrtle, Emmybeth didn't push Katherine. She just fell off the grapevine swing into the creek. No harm done. I reckon all of us took a tumble or two into that creek growin' up."

"Miss Hawkins, maybe you and Mama could draw the pattern for the stockings we're going to be working on for the nursing home. We can go ahead and get started on those this week. Sissy and Evelyn picked up the red felt last weekend when they went over to Johnson City shopping. I'd really like to go ahead and get the stockings finished, because there may be some Christmas presents we'd like to sew up for some of the shut-ins from church, and the fall just gets so busy, and gets away from us before we know it."

"Why, sure, Darlene. Esther, I can do this, you can just sit there and rest a spell."

"We haven't done anything yet, Myrtle, don't know as I need to rest."

"Mama, why don't you look through this embroidery thread, and see if we've got enough green to embroider some holly leaves on the stockings?"

Sometimes Momma sounds like a schoolteacher giving jobs to Miss Hawkins and Grandma.

"I bet that's Sissy and Evelyn coming up the driveway now. I'll just go see, well Mama, look out that porch window there. Junior's throwing dust coming up the driveway so fast. What's wrong with him? Sissy and Evelyn are turning in too. Let me step out here and see what's going on . . ."

Wonder what Junior's up to? He don't ever come here unless Daddy's home or sometimes, when him and Papaw Jack are out running around, they'll come by.

"Mama, come out here. Now!"

Grandma's getting up to go outside. Miss Hawkins too.

I wonder what they're doing. Maybe I can scoot up here and . . . "Lord, NO. Mama, I've got to go to him . . . Lord, Mama. Vernon can't . . . NO, NO! Mama, I've got to go."

I'm out of the cabinet and running out the door to Momma. There she is and Grandma's holding her up and Miss Hawkins is trying to give her a handkerchief.

"Emmybeth, where did you come from?"

"Momma, what's wrong? What are you crying for?"

I can feel the hot tears stinging my eyes now. I know there's just something awful wrong. I've never seen my Momma cry before.

"Momma, tell me!"

"Mama, you stay here with Emmybeth and go get Timmy."

"Momma, tell me, why are you cryin'?"

"Come here with me, Emmybeth. Your momma's got to go."

"No, Grandma, I wanna go with Momma. Where are you going Momma?"

"Mama, I gotta go now! Take Emmybeth and go down to your house with Timmy and Dad."

Momma's jumping into Junior's truck, and he's backing up real fast. I can't believe he's driving through the grass. Daddy never backs the car up on the grass like that. Junior's gonna be in big trouble when Daddy sees those tire tracks.

"Grandma, where's Junior taking Momma? Please tell me."

I wipe the tears with the back of my hand and look at her for an answer.

"Emmybeth, honey, there's been an accident down at the garage."

"Daddy's not hurt, is he Grandma? Not my daddy."

"Honey . . ."

"Grandma. What's the matter? Why won't you tell me?"

Mrs. Maiden and Mrs. Frazier have got out of their car and are just standing there looking at me and holding onto Grandma. Finally Miss Hawkins speaks up.

"Now child, just quit your blubbering. It won't help nothing. Least of all your daddy."

"Hush, Myrtle. Emmybeth, there's been an accident down at the garage. Something to do with a car battery blowing up. Now, I don't know how bad your Daddy's been hurt, but Junior says the ambulance is takin' him to the hospital in Johnson City. Your Papaw Jack's a ridin' in the ambulance with him. Now, we'll just go down and wait with Grandpop and Timmy . . ."

"NO! I want to go with Momma."

I take off running down the driveway. I'll catch Junior and Momma and ride with them. She should have let me come.

"EMMYBETH. Stop running. Come here, your Grandma can't run after you. Now, slow down, sweetie. Come on."

Mrs. Maiden catches the back of my shirt and pulls me into her arms, but I keep trying to wrench myself away. I gotta catch up with Momma and Junior.

"Mrs. Maiden, I gotta get to Johnson City. I need to go to the hospital. Let me go."

"Just calm down, Emmybeth."

"P . . . please, Mrs. Maiden. I gotta go, uh . . . with my Momma. Ssh . . . she needs me. Daddy needs m . . .me. I'm the oldest."

I'm cryin so hard now it's getting harder to talk and make them understand me.

"Come on now, Emmybeth. Just walk back up here to the house. If you'll just calm down, we'll see what your Grandma wants to do."

"I want to go to the hospital, Mrs. Maiden. I'll pay you. I've got $4.63 in my piggy bank. I'll give it to you for gas money, if you'll just take me."

"Emmybeth, I don't want your money. Just come up here and sit on the steps a minute. Evelyn, did you find those tissues in my purse? Emmybeth, just sit down, sweetie, and blow your nose. Now, take some slow breaths, and get yourself calmed down."

Grandma sits down beside me on the steps and takes my hand.

"Girls, I declare. I don't know what to do. I know I ought to stay here like Darlene told me to, but she's my daughter. I need to be with her. Junior won't know what to do . . . if . . . if . . ."

"If what, Grandma? If what?! Grandma, I want to go."

"Mrs. Phillips, if you want, I don't care to drive you and Emmybeth over to Johnson City."

Thank you, Mrs. Maiden; finally a grownup on my side.

"Come on Grandma. Mrs. Maiden says she'll take us. Come on, let's go."

"I don't know . . . I just don't . . ."

"Mrs. Phillips, I'll go with you and Sissy, and I'll take care of Emmybeth."

"Well . . . okay, Evelyn. Sissy, if you don't care to drive us . . . I guess if we could just stop by the house and tell Claude what's happened, then we could drive on over to the hospital and see what's going on."

"I'm comin' too, Esther. Just let me get my pocketbook. Reckon I oughta lock Darlene's door? You got a key?" Oh great.

Miss Hawkins has to butt in everywhere.

"Yes, Myrtle. Of course I gotta key, down at my house."

"Y'all wait just a minute. I'll be right back."

Well, shoot, Miss Hawkins will take forever to get back out here. But, I guess this is the only ride I'm gonna get to

Johnson City. I sure do hope it don't take long to get there. I just know there's something bad wrong with my Daddy. Grownups just don't cry, unless there's something really wrong.

Chapter 4

I can't believe I got crammed in this backseat between Grandma and Miss Hawkins. Just my luck. Miss Hawkins is holding onto her big old pocketbook for dear life. Knowing her, she probably thinks I'll steal something out of it if she turns loose of it. Nobody's hardly said a word at all since we left home. We stopped by Grandma and Grandpop's house, and Mrs. Maiden ran up to the door to tell Grandpop what happened, and that we were heading to the hospital. Grandma hollered out the back window for Grandpop not to say nothing to Timmy just yet. I think that's a good idea, since Timmy is just little. I'm just scared to death, but I'm gonna try real hard not to cry no more when I see Momma. I wonder if Daddy'll come home from the hospital today. I hope there's enough room in Junior's truck for Momma and Daddy and me and Papaw Jack; because I sure don't want to ride back to Ivy Creek with Miss Hawkins.

"Grandma."

"Yes, honey."

"Grandma, will they let my daddy come home today? Or will he have to stay in the hospital?"

"Honey, I don't know. Look there, there's the hospital. Turn here, Sissy."

"Yes, Mrs. Phillips. I see. Emmybeth, don't you worry. There are some really good doctors here. They'll get your daddy fixed up in no time flat."

"Sissy, why don't you let us all out at the front, and I'll help Mrs. Phillips find the Emergency Room while you park your car."

"Sounds good, Evelyn. I'll be right in as soon as I find a place."

"I'll come around and get your door Mrs. Phillips. Yours, too, Miss Hawkins. Just a minute."

"Lord, no, Evelyn. Just help Esther. I can manage."

Grandma's whispering something to Mrs. Frazier. I love Grandma, but I sure don't like it that she's being secretive. I know Daddy's hurt bad. They're just not telling me.

"Emmybeth, want to hold my hand?"

I reach out and take Mrs. Frazier's hand and walk between her and Grandma with Miss Hawkins following behind us. The doors to the hospital look like they're nine feet tall. I don't think I've been this scared in a long time. Maybe once when I was in second grade and Karen and me got to acting up in class real bad and our teacher said she'd send us to the principal's office if we didn't settle down quick. You can bet we settled down, and real quick just like she said to! Mrs. Frazier's headed over to the desk where it says Information. I'll bet the lady in the pink jacket will know where my daddy is.

"Excuse me. We're here to check on Vernon Johnson. The ambulance brought him in from Ivy Creek just a little while ago. Do you know where we should go?"

"Are you family?"

Grandma moves up to the desk.

"Yes, m'am. I'm his mother-in-law, and this here is his little girl."

"M'am, he's still in the Emergency Room, and the doctors are still working with him. I can't really tell you any more than that. You can go downstairs to the Emergency Waiting Room, but now, they won't let you go back into the room with him."

"How do we get down there?"

The lady in the pink jacket is directing Grandma and Mrs. Frazier. I feel like I just want to take off running, but it won't do me no good. I don't know where my daddy is . . . or my momma. I just want to find them. Why doesn't anybody understand that?

"Evelyn, reckon Sissy will be in here . . . oh, here she comes. Let's go see if we can find Darlene and Jack. Come on, Emmybeth."

"Mrs. Phillips, what did they tell you about Vernon?"

"We still don't know nothing, Sissy, except that he's in the Emergency Room. We're headin' that way right now." We start down a long hallway and get on the elevator. I swear every time I turn around I'm a bumping up against Miss Hawkins. She's really startin' to get on my nerves. Nobody wanted her to come anyway. She just has to butt into everything. The doors open and we get on the elevator and go down one floor to where the Emergency Room is. As soon as I get off the elevator I can see Momma and Papaw Jack sitting on a green couch. Junior must be off somewhere because I don't see him.

"Momma!"

"Emmybeth, how did you . . . Mama, how did y'all get here?"

"Now, Darlene, don't be upset with me, but Sissy offered to bring us over, seeing as how Emmybeth was so torn up, and I wanted to be here for you. How's Vernon? The woman upstairs said he's still in with the doctors. What's going on?"

"Oh, Mama, I just don't know what's happening. They were unloading Vernon out of the ambulance when Junior and me got here. Junior went to get Jack some coffee, just now. Anyway . . . Vernon's face was . . . well . . . Mama, it's his eyes."

Momma's looking at Grandma all concerned like grownups do, especially when they're trying not to say in front of you what's really happened.

"Emmybeth, want me to take you over here to the pop machine and get you something to drink? Or maybe some crackers to snack on?"

"No m'am, Mrs. Frazier. I'm okay."

I turn back and look at Momma real hard to see if I can tell what she's trying to say about Daddy. I guess I'll just out and out ask her.

"Momma, what's wrong with Daddy's eyes? You know you can tell me. I'm the oldest. Besides this is a real big place. I know they've got things to fix his eyes with here if that's what he needs."

"Emmybeth, you're here and there's nothing I can do about that now, but you're going to have to be a real big girl when I tell you what's happened. Come on over here and sit with us. Mama, girls, you can pull some chairs over here by the couch if you want."

Mrs. Maiden gets chairs for Grandma and Miss Hawkins. Her and Mrs. Frazier just stoop down by Momma. I still feel funny in my stomach. I just know something's real bad happened to Daddy. I squeeze in between Papaw Jack and Momma and the couch kinda squeaks when I sit back. Papaw Jack is stroking my hand when Momma starts talking.

"There was an accident at the garage this morning, just like Junior told us at the house. Seems that Vernon was outside pumping gas for Mrs. Cates, and some man, it wasn't anybody we know, just somebody passin' through, pulled into the parking lot, and got out to tell Vernon he was having trouble with his car. Vernon finished up with Mrs. Cates and she went on her way. Then, he went over to look under the hood of the man's car, right Jack?"

"Yes, Darlene, he just threw up the hood and started lookin' to see what was goin' on."

"And, well, it seemed that it was the battery getting ready to go out, because he could hear the motor sputtering, according to Jack. You know Vernon's always so careful. I can't believe that this . . ."

Momma starts crying again. Grandma's patting her, and there goes old Miss Hawkins digging for another handkerchief. Lordy sakes, wonder how many she carries in that big old pocketbook? I guess that's all she knows to do right now.

"Thank you, Miss Hawkins. Well, it seems that . . . it seems that when Vernon saw that it was the battery that was the trouble, because the alternator went out and the car died, he pulled his truck up next to it. He was going to boost it off, so he could get it into the bay . . . and then . . . then . . ."

Papaw Jack scoots forward a little and leans on his cane and starts talking to the ladies.

"I'll tell them, Darlene. That dadgum battery musta been old, and I guess Vernon didn't realize it. When Vernon hooked the jumper cables to it, that old battery just blew up, and his face was right down there beside it. I've always tried to warn him, and he's always been so careful, what with what happened to me at the garage, back there when he was a teenager. It just couldn't be helped. It was an accident. The man who owned the car feels just terrible. Darlene, he said to let him know what he could do . . . he's got insurance . . . he says. He's from over in Kingsport."

"Momma, Momma, what does he mean? What happened to Daddy?"

"Honey, the battery blew up in his face. Now, we don't know yet, just what that means. Junior was outside when it happened, and he got a bucket and started pouring water over your Daddy, just as quick as he could. Isn't that right Jack?"

"Yes, he did, Emmybeth. Junior did fer your Daddy what I couldn't do. I couldn't get out there to your daddy quick enough, but I hollered for Junior to run a bucket of water, and start pouring it over Vernon. I knowed that would help to get that old acid out of his eyes. Now, these doctor men here, they'll do the rest. Don't you worry none, Emmy."

Junior comes walking up with two cups of coffee.

"Here's your coffee, Jack. Just like you like it, strong and black. Ladies. I didn't realize y'all was a comin'. I'll go back and get you some coffee if you like."

"No, Jack I think we're all just fine. Miss Hawkins, Mrs. Phillips, Evelyn?"

Mrs. Maiden looks around to see if anyone wants anything. They're all just shaking their heads no and looking real sad. I'm trying real hard not to cry, but I think what they aren't telling me, is that Daddy's eyes may be hurting real bad. I hope the doctors give him something to make him stop hurting.

"Darlene, the doctor been out yet?"

"No, Junior, we're still just waiting."

"Junior, how's your mama doing out there at Sunny Meadows?"

For goodness sakes, why is Miss Hawkins talking to Junior just like there's nothing going on here? I snuggle in closer to Momma, and she puts her arm around me and starts talking just to me and not everybody else.

"Emmybeth, honey, does your Grandpop know where you all took off and went? What about Timmy? Oh Lord, he doesn't know, does he?"

"No, Momma. Mrs. Maiden stopped at Grandpop's, and told him we were coming to the hospital, and about the accident; but Grandma hollered and told Grandpop not to say nothing to Timmy. Momma, when will the doctor be out here?"

"I don't know, Emmybeth. I just don't know. I wish I did. I guess all we can do right now is pray that the doctors will take real good care of your daddy."

"Have you prayed yet, Momma?"

"Well, yes, I guess Emmybeth. I just keep saying, 'Please God, please take care of Vernon.' That's all I know to say right now."

I close my eyes, and hold them shut real tight. I sure do hope God can hear me over all the noise in this waiting room. Dear God, please take care of my daddy. He's been hurt real bad and I think there's something wrong with his eyes. Nobody's telling me for sure, but I bet you know. Reverend Cates says you know everything that's going on in the whole world. Please God, since you already know what's happened to my daddy, please, please, please do something about it. Amen.

About the time I open my eyes a tall man in a white coat is walking toward us.

"Mrs. Johnson, Mrs. Vernon Johnson?"

"Yes sir. I'm here. I'm Vernon Johnson's wife and this is his father, Jack Johnson."

The man nods at Papaw and motions to him not to stand up. I guess he can see Papaw Jack can't get up too good.

"I'm Dr. Daniels, I was with your husband here in the Emergency Room, and I've admitted him to the Intensive Care Unit. Does your husband have a regular physician?"

"Yes, Doctor Morgan, out in Ivy Creek, is who we usually see."

He writes down Doctor Morgan's name on his clipboard.

"Mrs. Johnson, I'm not going to mince words. Your husband has sustained a serious injury. I think the burns to his face, will heal eventually, and we can treat those here at this hospital; he won't have to be transferred to a burn hospital; but, m'am, I'm not sure we are going to be able to save his eyesight. Plain and simple, I think your husband may have lost his eyesight permanently. We're moving him to ICU. You'll be able to go back to visit with him twice a day. Someone will let you know when we get him situated. Just you and immediate family are allowed back in the ICU. Adults only. I'm sorry Mrs. Johnson. Your husband has a long road ahead of him."

The doctor turns around and walks away before Momma says anything. She's just staring as he goes down the hallway. That doctor's just lying. I know my Daddy will be able to see. It was just a little bit of battery acid and Junior washed it out of Daddy's eyes; just like Papaw Jack told him too. Daddy changes batteries all the time and he hasn't gone blind, yet. I hate that doctor.

"Mama . . . Jack . . ."

Momma's hugging herself real tight. She just stands there, with her head down and tears falling out of her eyes, onto the green and white tiles. She slowly lifts up her head, and stares down the hallway, where the doctor went. Maybe he'll come back. Maybe he'll say it was all a big mistake, and that it was somebody else's daddy that got blind; not mine. I just don't know what to do . . . even though I'm the oldest, and I got Mrs. Maiden to drive me all the way over here so I could help.

"Grandma, Grandma . . ."

Grandma gets up, and comes over to where I am, and pulls me up into her arms.

Oh, shoot! I tried so hard not to . . . but I think I'm gonna cry.

It seems like Grandma's arms were around me forever. I could feel her tears on my neck, all hot and wet. She just held me, and rubbed my back, until we both couldn't cry anymore, and then, she sat back down in her chair, and told me I could sit on her lap. I guess all these other people might think I'm too big of a girl to be sitting on my Grandma's lap; but I don't care . . . and it seems to help Grandma if I stay close to her. Momma finally sat back down on the couch with Papaw Jack; for the longest time she just stood staring after that doctor. It seems like even the grownups don't know what to do now.

"Well, younguns, anybody hungry? Lord knows a hospital this big, oughta have a cafeteria. If y'all come down with me, I reckon I'll just treat you to lunch. Any takers?"

"No, thank you, Miss Hawkins, I'm just going to stay here until someone comes and tells me they've got Vernon back in the ICU. Emmybeth, honey, are you hungry? Mama? Jack?"

Oh, Lord! Please, Momma, don't make me go alone with Miss Hawkins. She's liable to lose me in this hospital on purpose.

"No, Darlene, I'll sit here with you."

That's one down—Papaw Jack. Grandma, please don't let me down.

"Darlene, I'll tell you what, Evelyn and I'll go down with Miss Hawkins, and we'll take Emmybeth." Shoo! Thank you, Mrs. Maiden.

"Darlene, I'll just wait here with you and Jack, too. But now, Junior, what about you? Why don't you go on down?"

"Mrs. Phillips, I believe I will join the ladies for a bite. Jack, you sure you're all right? Want me to bring ya' anything?"

"No, no, I'll just stay here and wait with Darlene and finish my coffee. You go on now."

So, the whole lot of us get up, and start down the hallway looking for the cafeteria. Wouldn't you know Miss Hawkins is leading the way? I swear I bet the only reason she offered to buy everybody's lunch is so that she could go eat. My stomach's still feeling funny, but I reckon I could eat something.

"Emmybeth, you'll need to go wash your hands in the restroom. Evelyn and I will come with you to freshen up."

"Yes, m'am, Mrs. Frazier."

"Miss Hawkins, why don't you and Junior go on in, and you can just save us a seat at the table?"

"All rightee, Evelyn."

Okay, I think things are looking up. Maybe we can get rid of Miss Hawkins, but, wonder how I'll pay for my lunch?

"Emmybeth, honey, come on."

"Okay."

Mrs. Frazier and Mrs. Maiden go in the brown stalls and leave me by the sinks. Guess I'd better wash my hands and face, like Momma's all the time telling us to do before we eat. Mrs. Frazier and Mrs. Maiden come out, and go to fussing with their hair, and pulling little compacts and lipsticks out of their purses. I don't understand why women think they have to do that sort of thing. Not me. I don't want to have to spend that much time putting goop on my face, just so I can take it off again. Now, Karen, she's a different story. She's all the time wanting to experiment with putting on makeup and fixing her hair. When we were little, she always wanted to play "beauty parlor." Of course, Katherine already has lip gloss, and Love's Baby Soft perfume that she carries in her purse, and sprays every five minutes, 'til she just about chokes me to death; but not me.

"Emmybeth, you ready to get something to eat? Now, you just get in line with Mrs. Frazier and me. I'll pay for your lunch, honey. You just get anything you want to eat and some dessert, too, if you feel like it."

"Yes, m'am."

We walk out of the restroom single file and head on in to the cafeteria. I can see Miss Hawkins and Junior sitting at a table near the lunch line. It sorta looks like the school cafeteria, only bigger. Miss Hawkins and Junior must have got through the line quick, because they're already eating. Miss Hawkins has got all her little bowls and plates lined up on the table in front of her. Looks like she got enough to feed three people. Junior waves to us and motions to the empty chairs he's got for us at their table. Just my luck. I sorta like being with Mrs. Maiden and Mrs. Frazier. Not so much with Miss Hawkins.

"Now, Emmybeth, would you like some of the roast beef and mashed potatoes or it looks like they've got hamburgers there from the grill if you like? Whatever you want, just get it. Okay?"

"Yes, Mrs. Maiden. I think I'd just like a hamburger please, and some French fries too, if that's okay?"

"Okay, here we go. The condiments are over there Emmybeth."

"The what?"

"Oh, well, the ketchup, mustard, you know. The extras for your burger."

"All right. I'll just get some ketchup."

Golly, I guess Mrs. Maiden's used to being over here in Johnson City, and using words that we just don't use in Ivy Creek. Why not just say ketchup and mustard? Condiments? Whoever heard of such a strange word?

Everybody was real quiet like, with worried looks on their faces the whole time we was eating in the cafeteria. Mrs. Frazier got up and went to call her husband, and tell him where she was, so he wouldn't worry about her. Miss Hawkins said she'd call the preacher as soon as we all got back to Ivy Creek, and make sure he knows what had happened, so he could get the prayer chain going for daddy just as quick as possible. It's just like her wanting to deliver the news, but I bet everybody done knows. It's not like the ambulance comes to Ivy Creek every day.

Junior thought I couldn't hear him, when he was whispering to Mrs. Maiden, that this was gonna kill Jack. Mrs. Maiden said maybe we ought to talk about something else, like how to organize meals, or who was going to look after Timmy and me, so Momma could come to the hospital every day. Junior said he would take care of things down at the garage, with Papaw Jack, 'til Daddy could get on his feet again. That almost made me laugh. Nothing's wrong with Daddy's feet, it's his eyes they said was hurt.

Anyway, after we finished eating, we came on back to the Waiting Room with Momma and Grandma and Papaw Jack. It seems like they're gonna make us wait here forever. Nobody's come out and said anything about my daddy, since the doctor, the one I don't like too good, came out here and said Daddy wasn't going to be able to see again. I know that's not true. It's just not true and they can't make me believe it.

"Darlene, it's two o'clock. Reckon you ort'ta go back up there, and check at that desk again, and see what's goin' on? They ort'ta had Vernon back there in the ICU by now. It's been nearly two hours since that doctor talked to us."

"I know, Jack. I guess I should go check. I don't know why they're keeping us waiting like this. It's just punishment to wait."

"Now, Darlene, honey, why don't you just go up there and ask them when you can go back and see Vernon? You've got every right to know and we've certainly been waiting long enough."

"All right, Mama."

"Momma, I'm want to go with you."

"No, Emmybeth . . . well okay. I'm just going over here to the desk."

Momma and me walk over to where there's another lady in a pink jacket, sitting behind a desk. Momma clears her throat, to try and get the lady's attention.

"Excuse me. I'm Darlene Johnson, Vernon Johnson's wife. Dr. Daniels said they were moving my husband to the ICU, but that's been almost two hours ago. Do you have any information about him, it's Vernon Johnson from Ivy Creek? The ambulance brought him in . . ."

"Mrs. Johnson, all I can tell you is the nurse will let you know when he's situated. I'm just a volunteer. If you like, I'll call back and see what I can find out."

"Yes, m'am, that would be nice."

The lady picks up the phone and starts talking to someone back in the Emergency Room. I sure do wish they would let me see my Daddy. Surely they've got his eyes fixed by now.

"Mrs. Johnson, the nurse says she'll be right out to talk to you. Seems like they had to wait a bit for the ICU to send someone down to get your husband. He's upstairs, now, though. If you'll just give her a few minutes, she'll send someone out to give you the particulars."

"Okay. Thank you."

"Sure."

Gee whiz. All you do in this place is just sit down and wait, sit down and wait. Momma looks so bad, all of her makeup is gone off of her face, and it's all red and blotchy around her eyes.

I wish I could make her feel better.

Just then a nurse comes up to where we're all sitting.

"Mrs. Johnson. My name is Pam, and I work here in the Emergency Room, but I'm going to take you upstairs and show you where the ICU is. The next visiting time for family isn't until 5 o'clock this afternoon, but if you need to leave before then, since he's just got here, they may let you go back for a few minutes. I'm sorry only you and one other adult from the immediate family are allowed to go back."

The nurse looks around at all of us, like she can't figure out why there's this big bunch of people here. I guess that she doesn't understand that it's Thursday, and of course all these women were at our house for sewing circle, and they come over here to be with Momma.

"Darlene, you and Jack go on with her. M'am, would it be all right if this gentleman, here, goes and helps Jack get around?" Grandma motions toward Junior.

"Oh, don't worry about me Esther. I'll just use my cane and hold onto Darlene's arm here with the other hand. I can manage."

"We'll take the elevator up and the ICU is just a short way down the hall. I'll help you, sir."

The nurse and Momma head out with Papaw Jack to go see my Daddy. Nobody even asks about me, not even Momma. I guess I'll just have to wait here with Grandma and the other women . . . but I sure do wish I could see my Daddy. He's just got to be okay. He's too big and strong to be here in this hospital; and I'm too sad knowing he's gonna have to stay.

Chapter 5

I can't believe it's done been six weeks since Daddy had his accident. Momma's been to the hospital most every day, and me and Timmy have had to stay with Grandma and Grandpop just about all the time. That is, except for when I get to go over to Karen's and play, or when Mrs. Maiden and Mrs. Frazier come and get us to go to the store and get a treat.

The hospital don't allow children under twelve to visit, so me and Timmy haven't seen Daddy since the accident. Grandma says it wouldn't do us children no good anyway, to see our Daddy all bandaged up. We do get to talk to him on the phone, but just once a week. It's long distance to call to Johnson City from Ivy Creek, and that can get kinda expensive, according to Grandma. One time, when Mrs. Maiden and Mrs. Frazier rode over with Momma to the hospital, they took me and Timmy along with them. We got to wave to Daddy from the parking lot. We could just barely see him standing at his hospital room window. After that, the ladies took me and Timmy to the Miracle Mall, while Momma got her visit in with Daddy. I don't know why they call that place a miracle. According to my Sunday School teacher, miracles are for Jesus, and I didn't see him anywhere at the mall that day.

The sewing circle hasn't been meeting here at our house either. Seems that old Miss Hawkins has taken it upon herself to have Mrs. Maiden and Mrs. Frazier up to her house, and they've been working on the Christmas stockings for the nursing home people. I bet she's trying to steal them away from coming here. Momma keeps promising me that soon, everything will get back to normal. I start the fourth grade the Tuesday after Labor Day, so I don't have too many more weeks to be out of school. Maybe there'll be one more sewing circle before school starts so I can get caught up on all the news.

Seems like these days, every time I walk into the room when Momma's talking to Grandma, or to Papaw Jack, she just stops what she's saying. I just hate it when she does that; but I've been trying not to whine or bug her since Daddy's been hurt— since I'm the oldest. Of course, that means I've also had to try harder to be good to Timmy, and the Good Lord knows that's been awful hard on me. Timmy's just been staying with Grandpop most of the time, and that's okay with me. Grandma's been real good to me. She understands me most of all anyway.

"Emmybeth, Emmybeth, come in here for a minute. I've got some good news to tell you."

"Good news? What is it Momma?" I say as I head down the hallway to the kitchen.

"Emmybeth, there you are," Momma says as I walk through the doorway.

"What is it?" I repeat.

"Emmybeth, that was your Daddy on the telephone just now. Seems that the doctor just told him he can come home, first thing tomorrow morning. Isn't that exciting news, honey?"

"It sure is, Momma. Can I come to the hospital with you, please, pretty please?"

"We'll see, Emmybeth. But, honey, right now we've got a lot of work to do to get ready, if he's coming home in the morning. I'll need you to help me. Let's see . . . we'll wash the bed sheets, and hang them out on the clothesline, so the bed will smell fresh and nice, just like your Daddy likes it . . . and . . . I'll send you and Timmy over to Grandma's garden to get some ripe tomatoes, and pick us a mess of green beans. You know how much your Daddy likes them. I'll cook them for lunch tomorrow."

"But, Momma, when Daddy comes home is he going to be able to see? How's he going to eat?"

"Now, Emmybeth, I've told you and Timmy already. No, Daddy can't see and he won't ever be able to see. But he's just fine. He's still your Daddy, just like always, and we'll get by just fine. Don't you be saying anything to him about not being able to see, Emmybeth. Your Daddy's a proud man. He's gonna be just fine. Just you wait. Now, go on, get Timmy and y'all go down to the garden. Tell Grandma and Grandpop your Daddy's coming home in the morning. Now, scoot."

"Yes, m'am."

I am happy that Daddy's coming home, but wonder why I have this funny feeling in my stomach every time Momma says that he's not gonna be able to see anymore? How will he know how to get around the house, and what will I say to him when he can't see to sit in his chair, or get a Coca-Cola out of the refrigerator? I just don't know how I'm supposed to act when he gets home.

"Timmy, you gotta come outside with me. Momma says you've got to go to Grandma's garden with me, and pick beans and gather tomatoes. Daddy's coming home tomorrow morning and Momma wants to fix his favorite foods for lunch when he gets here."

"Emmybeth, I don't wanna go to the garden. It's hot outside."

"Come on, Timmy. Quit whining. I'm gonna tell Momma if you talk back to me. I'm the oldest."

"Oldest, smoldest. You're a pain in the butt, Emmybeth."

"I'm warning you, Timmy. You'd better come. Right now, young man."

There, that'll get him. That's what Momma says when she means business.

"Okay, okay."

It really is hot outside today. Timmy keeps kicking up dust as he walks. Of course, that has a lot to do with the way he drags his feet because he don't like to go to the garden. Now, I think it is kinda fun in the garden. I like helping Grandma plant seeds in the spring, and then watching for the plants to spring up through the ground. I even think it's fun to pick the beans and gather the tomatoes. It's just like hunting for Easter eggs when you find a ripe, red tomato underneath a bunch of green ones. Timmy thinks I'm crazy when I say stuff like that—so, I just don't tell him. He's hardly worth talking to most of the time anyway.

"Here, Timmy, take this pan and you start picking on this row of beans, and only pick the ones that are full—remember, like Grandpop showed you. I'm going in and tell Grandma and Grandpop that Daddy's coming home in the morning."

"Why do you get to go in and I have to start pickin' stupid beans?"

"Because Momma said so, dopey, and you'd better not stick out your tongue out at me, or I will tell on you."

"Okay, okay."

I'm pretty sure he will stick his tongue out when I turn around and start toward the house. But like I said, he's hardly worth talking to; so I just ignore him.

"Grandma," I call out as I head through the back door to the kitchen. It always smells so good in here. This morning it smells like pancakes. I guess that's what they had for breakfast.

"Grandma, where are you? I've got good news for you and Grandpop."

"Emmybeth, I'm back here in my bedroom stripping the sheets off the bed to wash. Come on back, honey. Tell me your good news."

I head down the hallway to Grandma's bedroom.

"Grandma, Daddy's coming home in the morning. Momma sent me and Timmy over here to get some beans and tomatoes out of the garden to cook for his lunch tomorrow. I'm so excited . . . I guess. Anyway, I've got to get back outside and help Timmy, or he'll be fussin'."

"Slow down, child. Grandpop's out in the shed. He'll see Timmy and help him. You sit down here, and tell me all about this news, while I put the clean sheets on the bed.

Now, why do you say you guess you're excited? Emmybeth, you ought to be excited. Why, it's been six weeks since you've seen your Daddy, and I know he misses you and Timmy real bad. What's wrong?"

That's Grandma. She can always tell what I'm thinking. It's just kinda hard to put it into words . . . even for Grandma.

"Grandma, I, uh. Oh, it don't matter. I'd better go help Timmy. He'll tattle to Momma if I don't, and I don't want her to be bothered. I'll just go . . ."

"Emmy, now, you just wait a minute. Grandpop's outside and he can help Timmy. You tell me what's wrong. I know something's been a' botherin' you. You can tell me, Emmybeth."

Well, shoot. There go the tears falling out of my eyes. Maybe if I squeeze my eyes shut real tight. No, there I go with a big, fat sob. Just like a baby.

"Emmy, Emmybeth, now honey. It'll be okay. Grandma's here."

Grandma sits down on the bed beside me and holds me real tight. We sorta rock and sway. I guess I am a big ole' baby. It's a long time before I stop crying. When I finally slow down and get a hold of myself, the words begin to tumble out of my mouth, before I can make any sense of them in my head.

"Grandma, it's just so hard to think what it's gonna be like with a blind Daddy. I mean . . . I mean . . . it's just so awful to think he'll be blind forever; and wherever we go people will be lookin' at him and he won't know it; but I will. And I'm probably gonna be punished by the Good Lord because I'm ashamed of my Daddy; and I know it's wrong, and I don't know what to do. But I ain't never, I mean, I have never, Momma says don't say 'ain't'; but anyway, I've never even seen a blind person, except on TV."

"Emmybeth, honey, just settle down. Lord have mercy. Take a deep breath. That a girl. You are not going to be punished for nothing, Emmybeth. Honestly, child, sometimes I don't where you get such ideys in your head. Now, you're just a worryin' and thinkin' way too much about things you don't have no control over. Your Daddy is blind now, and that's a fact. We can't change it. If people don't have any better sense than to stare at him, then, so what? If they're that ignorant, there's not a thing you can do about it. You love your Daddy, just the same as always, and he loves you. I promise you, Emmybeth, with a love that big and good, you and your Daddy'll be all right. It'll be hard, especially at first, for all of us. But we're not quitters, and we're not gonna let this get the best of us, any of us. Okay?"

"Well . . . I guess . . . if you say so, Grandma." I don't sound too sure, even to myself.

"Besides, me and Grandpop will be there tomorrow when your Daddy gets home. You just stick close to me, if you get to feelin' unsure of yourself, okay? Grandma always takes care of her girl. You know that, don't you?"

"Yes, Grandma."

"You run on outside, Emmybeth, and see what Timmy and Grandpop are gettin' into while I finish making up this bed. If they're not pickin' beans and gatherin' tomatoes, you come get me and I'll straighten them out!"

"Okay, Grandma," I say as I run outside with the first smile I can remember having in a real long time. That Grandma of mine. She's the best.

Momma woke me up at the crack of dawn this morning.

I guess that's why I'm so sleepy, now, riding toward Johnson City, with Momma and Junior, to pick up Daddy from the hospital. Momma let me come, but Timmy had to stay behind with Grandma and Grandpop at our house. Grandma's working on getting lunch ready for Daddy when we get back. Momma brought Junior along in case she needs help getting Daddy's stuff to the car. He's driving our car which seems strange to me.

Momma can drive. She just don't like to—I guess that's one more thing that'll change. Daddy won't be able to drive our car anymore; that'll seem funny to see him in the passenger's seat and Momma at the wheel. I don't think I've ever seen a woman drive a man in a car. Something about that just don't seem right.

"Emmybeth, we're almost there. Are you excited, honey?"

"Yes, Momma."

"It'll be so good to have Daddy home again. Just like it used to be."

"Uh, huh. I mean, yes, m'am."

I don't know why Momma keeps saying that—it won't be like it used to be. Maybe coming this morning was a big mistake. Now I'm almost wishing I was back home with Grandma . . . even Timmy . . . well, not so much Timmy; but I sure do wish I was with Grandma. There's the hospital, just ahead on the left.

"Emmybeth, now you remember what I told you. Your Daddy is just the same. Okay?"

"Yes, Momma."

"Darlene, I'll just pull up here and wait in the patient pickup lane. You know them nurses'll bring Vernon down in a wheelchair; hospital rules. That's how it was when my mama was here with her heart spell last year. I'll help him git over into the car when y'all git down. All right?"

"Okay, Junior. You're probably right about them bringing him down. Emmy, you come with me while Junior waits right here. We'll be back in a jiffy, Junior, and we'll have Vernon with us. Won't we Emmy?"

"Sure, Momma."

I haven't been in the hospital since the day Daddy got hurt. I sure do wish I could feel more excited, but I'm just too scared right now. Momma leads me through the doors into the lobby.

"Emmybeth, you'll have to sit right here, while I go get your Daddy. I'm going to tell the lady at the desk, you see the one in the pink jacket there, I'm going to tell her I've got to go up and get your Daddy; and I'll be right back down. I promise. Now just don't talk to any strangers and sit right here in front of the desk. Okay?"

"Momma, why can't I go up?"

"Now, Emmy, you know the rules here. I told you before we left home that you'd have to sit down here for a few minutes. You're a big girl. You'll be all right. Besides, I'm going to make sure that lady knows your name, and she'll keep an eye on you. Please be a good girl about this Emmy. I need to go on up and get your Daddy checked out, so we can go home."

"Okay."

Momma goes over and talks to the lady in the pink jacket. She smiles and waves at me. I wave back, so as not to upset Momma. Boy, me and my big mouth. I really don't want to be here at all now. Of course, I could be stuck out in the car with Junior. He's all right. It's just that sometimes I feel like he talks to me like I'm three years old, and it just gets all over my nerves. Maybe Momma is right, and I just need to try harder to be nice to people. I look over at the lady in the pink jacket and smile at her, for real this time. I am going to try harder. It couldn't hurt anything and maybe it will help me be a better soldier for the Lord. I hope so. I wonder why it is that when grownups say 'it'll be just a minute,' it seems like it's forever. I'll just sit back here and close my eyes for a little bit. I really am so sleepy . . . Momma got me up so early.

"Emmy, well I declare, Emmy . . . wake up. Here's your Daddy, Emmy."

I must have drifted off for a little while. When I open my eyes Momma is standing beside my chair and there's a man in a wheelchair, with a nurse standing behind him. Oh, no, that's my Daddy.

"Emmybeth, is that you, honey? Daddy's girl is sleepy this morning, aren't you?"

"Emmy, give your Daddy a kiss. He's missed you an awful lot."

I stand up and go over to the wheelchair. He's holding a funny looking white cane between his knees. I guess that's something blind people use.

"Uh . . . hello . . . Daddy."

Do I tell him it's me? Oh, no. I really don't know what to do. Please, Jesus. Help me.

"It's okay, Emmybeth. I bet these new-fangled sunglasses look funny to you, and this walking stick, don't they? Don't worry, Emmy girl. You'll get used to them. I have."

Daddy's wearing dark, black sunglasses that wrap around his face. He looks like some kind of spaceman. His skin's all red and funny looking, and I can see the scars from the burns that run back to his ears. Momma didn't tell me. I didn't know. She kept saying it would be the same. I knew she was wrong. But, I'll be brave. After all, I am the oldest.

"Now, Mrs. Johnson," the nurse says to my momma, "It's important you continue using the creams on Mr. Johnson's skin, just like we've shown you. Here's a prescription and the appointment card for his follow up here. Remember, it's also important that you go to your regular doctor as well. I trust you can make that appointment soon."

"Oh, yes m'am. I already have. Dr. Morgan will be seeing Vernon next week. Thank you again for everything—all the other nurses, too. You'll make sure the night shift nurses get the cookies I made for them?"

"I will, and day shift will enjoy ours as well. Well, Mr. Johnson, I guess this is good-bye."

"Yes, m'am. I'm mighty grateful to all of you here, and what you did for me."

"We're just doing our jobs. You take care now. Good-bye."

"Bye."

Daddy holds up his hand awkwardly. I can tell he's not sure where to aim his wave. Momma pushes him through the doors and out to the parking lane where Junior is waiting. I follow along. Daddy doesn't say anything else as we go toward the car. He's got such a mad face on—this just isn't like my Daddy.

"Vernon, Junior's got the car here waiting on us."

"Darlene, why did you . . ."

"Vernon," Junior says real loud to Daddy. Wonder if he thinks Daddy's lost his hearing, too?

"Hey, Junior. What's going on?"

"Nothing much, Vernon," he says, still a bit too loud. Gee whiz. How are the kids supposed to know what to do, if even the grownups don't know how to act around Daddy?

"Junior, would you open the trunk, so we can put Vernon's suitcase back there? Now, Vernon, honey, be careful. I'll help you."

"Darlene, I'm not helpless."

"Oh, Vernon, you know how fussy these women can be. Now, just git holdt of my arm there and I'll help ya' git in the front seat here. Darlene, you and Emmybeth just go on around, and git in the backseat. I'll git the suitcase and whatnot and put it in the trunk."

Momma gets into the backseat of the car and I slide in behind her. I scoot over to sit close to her, and she puts her arm around me. I take hold of her hand and give it a tight squeeze. Junior finishes getting Daddy situated and gets in the driver's seat and starts the engine. We ride along for several minutes in silence. It's just so different now. Junior finally breaks the silence and starts talking to Daddy about what's going on down at the garage. Daddy listens and talks to him, but he just doesn't seem the least bit interested in talking to me and Momma. Why it used to be that on Sunday afternoon when me, Timmy, Momma and Daddy would go out for a drive, Daddy would tell corny jokes and make us laugh. Momma would roll her eyes and say, "Oh, Vernon, stop that nonsense," but she would always wind up laughing too. Sometimes Daddy would sing Elvis Presley songs and look at Momma all goofy like. She'd act like she didn't like it, but you could tell she did. It don't look like Daddy's gonna do no singing today.

"Emmy, I bet Grandma's got those beans cooked, and I think she was going to fry a chicken, too. That's your favorite, isn't it sweetie?"

"Yes, Momma. Momma, when are we gonna go shopping for school clothes? It's getting close to time for school to start; not that I mean we have to go today. I's just afraid, well, maybe you'd forgot."

"Oh, no, Emmybeth. I didn't forget. It's just with what, well, we'll go just as soon as we can, honey. I wouldn't ever forget something like that—why you'll be in the fourth grade this year. We'll have to get you some big girl outfits. We'll do it soon. You need some new shoes too. We'll get it done, Emmybeth. I promise."

"Look, Momma, there's Timmy and Grandpop waving on the porch. Look, Daddy."

Oh, shoot. I can't believe I said that.

Daddy turns his head toward the backseat and just smiles a sad, crooked smile.

"Vernon, she didn't mean nothing."

"No, no. It's okay. I know what she meant."

I could just die. Why did I have to go and say something so stupid? Momma squeezes me tight to her, but I don't feel any better. This is just too hard. It'll never be right again. Things have changed. I can just feel it in my bones.

We get inside and everybody makes a big fuss over Daddy. He's polite enough, but he just don't talk as much as he used to do. Junior left to get back down to the garage and keep it open for the afternoon, since Papaw Jack's here for Daddy's homecoming lunch. Daddy thanked Junior real nice like, but he hardly answered anybody else when they was asking him questions about being in the hospital and his doctor's appointments and stuff like that. He tried to pat Timmy on the head, but he missed. Timmy didn't seem to mind. He just squealed and hugged Daddy's legs, and then grabbed his cane wanting to play with it like it was a sword. Momma told him to give in back to Daddy, "right now," so, he did; but, he wasn't too happy about it.

Grandma's got a big meal on the table. She fixed the beans that me and Timmy picked, and has our big blue platter filled with red and yellow tomatoes. She did fry a chicken, which is my favorite. Daddy likes it too. She's even made a chocolate pie. Normally, when it's just Momma and me and Timmy for lunch, we just have grilled cheese sandwiches, or sometimes peanut butter and banana, with the banana all smashed up in the peanut butter. Timmy likes it that way.

"Daddy, why don't you turn thanks for us, and then we'll dig into this wonderful lunch Mama fixed. Vernon, I know you didn't get any cooking like this at the hospital."

"No, I didn't," Daddy just stares straight ahead, and don't even turn his head toward Momma. That just don't seem polite, even if he can't see her.

"Darlene," Grandpa nods his head to Momma and motions for her to take her seat next to Daddy's chair at the head of the table.

"Dear Heavenly Father. We're here today to enjoy this wonderful meal Esther has prepared for us; but we're also here to give thanks, Lord, for bringing Vernon home to us. He's traveled a long road back to us, Lord, but we know you've been with him every step of the way. We want to thank you, Lord and praise you for it. Bless Darlene and these children as they continue to help Vernon each and every day. We ask that you bless those less fortunate than us, and help us to help them in any way we can. Bless this food to our nourishment and our bodies to your service. It's in your Son's name we ask all these things. Amen and amen."

"Amen," everyone around the table chimes in . . . except my daddy.

As soon as the prayer ends, everybody starts passing the food around and filling up their plates. Momma has to help Timmy, but I can manage fine on my own.

"Claude, you are a lucky man having such a fine cook as Esther is here."

"That shore is the truth, Jack."

"Darlene, let me get up and get Timmy's milk. You need to eat your food before it gets cold."

"Mama, I'm fine. Just sit still. Emmybeth, I'll fill up your glass too. You didn't drink any milk this morning. I guess you were just excited."

Yeah. Excited. She's just not seeing things the way they are these days. Can't Momma see how scared I am? She comes back in and fills up mine and Timmy's glasses and sits back down.

"Uh, Vernon," Papaw Jack clears his throat and starts talking to Daddy.

"What is it, Dad?"

"Well, I's jest a thinkin'. When is it you reckon you'll be comin' back into the garage? Now, I don't want to be tellin' tales outta school, that Junior's a fine mechanic, and he sure has stepped up to the plate these past six weeks. But . . . well, but, it's jest this, Vernon, Junior ain't no businessman, you know that's the truth. I've done my best to keep check on things, and I'm down there most every day anyway. It's jest that your business needs tendin' to, son. And what with cold weather comin' on, you know it'll be here before we know it, I can't be there all the time. It jest hurts my old legs too much to git out in the cold, and I won't be able to be there. You need to git back down there and oversee your business, son.

Junior will still be there workin', I even think he's takin' to workin' everyday, now that he's tried it. And maybe you can even git you a high school kid to help with pumpin' the gas of the afternoon, and doin' clean up and stuff. I's jest wonderin' . . . about . . . it."

Papaw Jack's words just trail off and disappear into the air. Everybody's real quiet now and looking toward my daddy. He starts laughing a real strange laugh. I've never heard him laugh like this. Usually when Daddy laughs, it makes me want to laugh too. This laugh just makes me scared.

"Well, Daddy. I see you've got it all figured out for me. It was my eyes that got burned up, Daddy. Not my brain. I know the business needs tending to . . . but do you really think I can oversee it? What a joke, old man. Me . . . a blind man . . . in case you haven't noticed. I can't oversee nothing. It's just darkness for me; from here on out. Yeah, a blind mechanic, good one, Daddy. How long did it take for you to think up that one? Ha. Ha. Ha."

"Now, Vernon, I'm sure your Daddy's just trying to help. Isn't that right, Jack? Vernon, honey, please don't get yourself so worked up," Momma says as she leans toward Daddy. She starts to put her hand out, like she's going to pat Daddy's arm; but then, she doesn't, and lays her hand down on the table.

I feel sorry for Papaw Jack. I ain't never seen Daddy like this. Daddy leans in real close to the table and points his finger toward Papaw Jack; well, sort of. I think that's where he means to point it.

"If you think for one minute I'm going down there to be the laughingstock of Ivy Creek, then you're a crazy old fool,

Daddy. I don't have to do it, and I'm not going to do it. You take care of it. I'm through. I'm done in. I'm a blind man now. Good for precious little. All of y'all can just get used to it. Lord knows I've had to."

I look over and see Timmy bury his head in Grandpa's arm and start to cry.

"Darlene," Grandpop stands ups and lifts Timmy from his chair, "I'm gonna take Timmy in the front room, and get him quieted down. We'll eat our lunch later, won't we Timmy?"

Timmy just starts to cry for real now, and Grandpop carries him into the living room. Papaw Jack just looks down at his plate and starts pushing his food around with his fork. I don't know what to do. I guess I'll just try to eat too. I don't think I'll be able to swallow anything, though. I know it won't go past the lump in my throat; it's a big as a goose egg.

"Vernon, please quit raising your voice. Mama's made this nice lunch. Let's just try and enjoy it before it gets cold. We'll figure out all this stuff later," Momma says.

I know she's trying to keep the peace. That's what Grandma says my momma always tries to do. Grandma takes a slice of cornbread from the pan and starts to butter it for me. I don't need her to, but I just let it go, for once. Momma reaches for the cornbread too.

"Here, Vernon, you want me to butter some cornbread for you? Mama made it just special . . ."

"Butter my cornbread. Butter my cornbread! No, goddammitt! I don't need you to butter my goddamn bread, like I'm some goddamn youngun," Daddy yells louder than before.

He stands up and tries to grab his cane from where it was leaning against the table; but he misses it; and instead the chair goes flying backwards, and so does the cane. He turns around and starts to step away, but instead he trips over the chair and lands hard on the kitchen floor.

"Vernon! No, watch, Vernon," Momma cries out too late.

Daddy is all tangled up now. His cane is halfway across the room. Momma gets up to try and help him up. My daddy's crying now and so am I. Oh, no . . . oh, no . . . I'm so scared. I've gotta go pee, right now, but Momma motions to me to stay in my chair. I'm not sure I can hold it. I place my leg underneath me and press hard against myself to try to keep myself from peeing. The sobs are coming so fast now, I can't tell if it's me, or my daddy crying.

"Goddamn, Darlene. Goddammit to hell!"

I've never heard my Daddy curse like this. Momma helps him to stand up, and picks up the white cane, and hands it to him. Daddy's still sobbing. The tears just keep coming down his cheeks from behind the black glasses. A long string of snot is coming out of his nose, and he don't even seem to care. He keeps sobbing and cursing as Momma helps him down the hallway toward their bedroom. They go in and I hear Momma close the door behind her.

"Esther, I'm gonna go to the front room and check on Claude and Timmy."

Papaw Jack gets up and shuffles out of the kitchen toward the living room. Grandma leans over to hug me, but I pull away from her. She tries to pat me.

"No, Grandma, no! Just go away and leave me alone."

Grandma pulls my chair around toward her and sees my predicament. There's a puddle underneath my chair, and I could just die from embarrassment. Grandma never says a word. She just helps me to my feet and puts her arm around me as we head toward my bedroom. When we get to my room, Grandma helps me out of my wet clothes and finds me some dry ones. I lay down on my bed, and turn toward the wall. Grandma strokes my hair while I cry . . . until finally, I fall asleep.

Chapter 6

"I'm just not gonna stand for it, Darlene."

Grandma's fussing about my daddy again to Momma—
I swear, this has been going on every day for the past week
or so. Momma never has mentioned it to me—how Daddy
acted the day he came home from the hospital. I've just let it
be; it's not something I want to talk about too much, either.
Grandma's not said anything to me about it directly; but, she
has been extra special nice to me, and hugs on me, all the
time, when she's around.

We had to come down here to Grandma and Grandpop's
this morning, so Momma could help Grandma can the last
of the tomatoes. Timmy and Grandpop are in the den,
watching game shows of course. I've been helping Momma
and Grandma. It's my job to screw the rings on the jars, once
Momma pours the tomatoes in—we haven't got to that part
yet. So, I'm just supposed to sit here, I guess, and read my
Nancy Drew book. Grandma and Momma are still peeling
tomatoes on the screen porch.

"Darlene," Grandma's trying to talk soft-like to Momma, but she's not being particularly good about keeping her voice down this morning. I can hear her through the screen.

"Darlene, I know you're gonna get mad at me, but I've just got to speak my piece."

"Mama, please, don't start in on this again. Emmybeth might hear you."

"Darlene, she's a readin'. Now, look, if Vernon wants to sit in the bedroom, with the lights out and the drapes drawn the rest of his life, it's his business; but he's not gonna make you and Timmy and Emmybeth prisoners too. It's just not healthy for them younguns, or you, for the matter."

"Mama, please," Momma's starting to cry, I can tell, "It's not even been two weeks since he got home from the hospital. You're just going to have to try harder to understand what he's going through."

"I understand all right. I got the full picture the day he come home and got the whole house in an uproar, with his goin's on. He got Emmybeth and Timmy plum torn up, Darlene. Them younguns don't need that kinda display. It's not good for them, and it's not good for you, either."

Lordy, it seems all anybody ever does anymore is fuss about one thing or another; except my daddy. He just don't say nothin' at all. Sometimes Timmy goes into his bedroom and sits and talks to him. I've just been in there once or twice, and that was when Momma sent me in with a glass of Coca-Cola for Daddy. I go in and I come out as quick as I can. It's dark in the bedroom, for one thing; and Daddy looks scary to me sitting there in the dark, wearing those big, black glasses. He smells funny, too, now; not like Old Spice, like he used to.

Maybe it's all those creams Momma has to rub on his face, or, it could be that he's only taking a bath every other day or so. He just sits there in his t-shirt and Dickie work pants, drinking Coca-Cola and listening to WJCT-AM, the country music station out of Johnson City.

Momma still keeps saying everything is fine. She's even promised to take me clothes shopping on Saturday. We're going to go to Sears in Johnson City. It's still downtown, not in the Miracle Mall, yet. It will be before Christmas, though. They just have to finish building the store in the mall. The new Sears entrance was covered with black plastic when Mrs. Maiden and Mrs. Frazier took Timmy and me to the mall, while Daddy was still in the hospital. Momma's said she's got to get some clothes for Timmy, too. She don't know it, but when we got down here to Grandma's house this morning, I saw Grandpop give her a hundred dollar bill to buy our school clothes with. She looked all teary eyed when he done it.

Timmy's gonna be in kindergarten at Apple Grove Presbyterian Church, up the road, toward Johnson City. That's where I went, too. You don't have to go to kindergarten, but Momma says it's good for you to go. It gets you prepared for first grade. It only costs thirteen dollars a month to go there. I guess Timmy'll still get to go. I can't believe Momma took money from Grandpop for our school clothes. Daddy'll really blow up if finds that out . . .

"Honey, you just need to get out of that house. It just kills me to know you're up there everyday, waiting on him, trying to keep him pacified, so's he won't get mad."

"Mama, I'm down here, now; and I've already promised to take Emmybeth clothes shopping on Saturday; that should count for something."

"Yes, but you need to get back to your normal life, Darlene. You need stuff, like, getting back to the sewing circle, for one. That's what you and me will do. We need to go up to Myrtle's in the morning. You know she's already scheduled it at her house, again. We'll just let her and the girls know that next week we're meeting back at your place. School will be back in next Tuesday, so that'll work out fine. Now in the morning, Emmybeth can come with you and me, and Timmy can stay here with Claude. And Vernon can just sit up there in the dark."

"Mama," my momma sounds kind of exasperated, now.

"Well, I didn't mean any disrespect, Darlene."

"I know. It's just . . ."

"It's just nothin'. It's decided. Now, help me carry this pot full of tomatoes to the stove."

Grandma and Momma come through the screen door into the kitchen where I'm sitting.

"Emmybeth, you make sure you get up early in the morning and get ready. You're comin' to the sewing circle tomorrow at out Miss Hawkins's." Grandma says with a wink.

That's a girl, Grandma. Maybe everything will get back to normal, soon. I sure do hope so.

It's Thursday morning. Timmy's with Grandpop, and I'm in the backseat of the car, heading toward Miss Hawkins's house, with Momma and Grandma. Daddy's in his and Momma's bedroom at home; just like Grandma said he would be—lights out, drapes drawn, and listening to WJCT-AM playing on the radio. Momma is driving us out to Milk Hollow Road to Miss Hawkins's place. Grandma's been complaining to Momma about Miss Hawkins takin' over the sewing circle, while Daddy was in the hospital. Momma's asked her to please not be starting anything this morning. Grandma said she wouldn't, but I don't think she meant it.

We drive up the long, gravel driveway to Miss Hawkins's house. I've been out here once or twice before. The best I remember the house smells like Vick salve. But, that may have been because when I was out here last time, it was when Old Man Hawkins, Miss Hawkins's daddy, died. I guess when he was about to die they rubbed him with Vicks salve. Anyway, the house sure does look fancy. We have to drive up the gravel driveway pretty far before you can begin to see the house.

It's two stories tall and has a big porch that wraps all the way around both sides of the house. It's not a brick house like ours; it's painted white, with black shutters. The porch is so big, it's got ceiling fans. There's concrete planters, painted white and full of red geraniums. The planters are lined up across the front of the porch, in a line, just like a bunch of soldiers. They sit on top of the wall that goes around the porch.

This would be a good place to come and play, if old Miss Hawkins wasn't so hateful. Momma said to mind my manners while I'm here today, so I'll have to try hard. I thought she was gonna back out at the last minute and not let me come, but Grandma wouldn't allow her to. I guess you always have to mind your mother; even when you're a grownup and have children of your own, like my momma.

Momma pulls up behind Mrs. Maiden's car. We all three get out and walk up the sidewalk, onto the porch. Grandma steps up to the door and knocks. Momma and me are just standing back behind her. I can see Miss Hawkins coming through the dim light, walking down the hallway toward us. She opens the door and looks a little bit surprised.

"Well, I never. Look here younguns," she yells over her shoulder back into the hallway. "It's Esther, and she's brought Darlene and her girl. Come on in. Let me hold the door open for you."

It's just like her to make a big fuss. She acts like she didn't just see us at church last Sunday.

"Sissy and Evelyn's already out in the dining room; they're having a piece of my homemade caramel cake and a cup of coffee before we start. Just come on down the hall, here with me. Darlene, it's good to have you back. I's just saying to the other girls, it's time you be joining us."

"Thank you, Miss Hawkins. I'm glad to be here today."

I guess even my momma's not above a little white lie. She sure didn't act like she wanted to come here.

"Darlene," Mrs. Maiden gets up and comes over to hug my momma, "It's so good to see you. You too, Mrs. Phillips. Emmybeth, how are you? Excited about school starting next week?"

"Yes, m'am. Well, sorta. It was nice being out for the summer."

"I know, sweetie."

"Darlene, come here so I can hug you, too," Mrs. Frazier gets in on the act.

Everybody is talking at once—funny how they can do that, and still understand each other.

"Darlene, maybe Emmybeth would like to get her cake and go out on the porch there yonder?"

Oh, shoot! Of course Miss Hawkins would think of someway to get rid of me. I look toward Grandma for some support, but there's not much she can do.

"Of course, Miss Hawkins. Emmybeth brought her Nancy Drew mystery to keep her occupied. She'll be fine out on the porch. Won't you, Emmybeth?"

"I . . . guess so, Momma."

Just then an old lady comes through the swinging doors from the kitchen. They're those old fashioned swinging doors, like you see in Miss Kitty's saloon on *Gunsmoke*. That's funny. Miss Hawkins sure is no Miss Kitty. The old woman is carrying a china pot and her hands are shaking real bad. I hope that's not hot coffee in there, but I've got a feeling it is. Everybody might want to watch out when she comes toward them.

"Girls, y'all remember Miss Trula? You know, she's been our hired girl since my mama and daddy got married and come here to live with Mammy and Pappy Hawkins. She even helped Mama to raise up all us younguns. That right, Miss Trula?"

"That's right, uh huh."

"Now that all of my brothers and sisters have moved away or passed on, it's just me and Miss Trula."

No wonder. If Miss Hawkins was my sister, I'd die or move away too. Oops. Sorry, Jesus.

"Miss Trula, cut Emmybeth a piece of that cake. I put a paper plate there on the sideboard for hers. Emmybeth, you just follow Miss Trula, on out to the kitchen, she'll get you some milk and show you out to the porch," Miss Hawkins dismisses me, like she's a schoolteacher and it's the end of the day.

I throw one last pleading look toward Grandma, but then I see Momma raise her eyebrows and purse her lips as she motions me toward the kitchen. Grandma looks at me and smiles a sweet smile, but I guess I'm out of here. Well, shoot. I'll never get caught up on all the gossip, I think, as I follow Miss Trula through the swinging doors out to the kitchen.

"They said your name is Emmybeth. That right? That's a real nice name. Just sit here while I get you some milk to have with your cake. Then I'll show you outside."

Miss Trula seems nice enough. After all, she did cut me a big slab of the homemade caramel cake. I bet if Miss Hawkins had cut it, it would have been a sliver. She gets a jelly glass out of the cabinet beside the stove and gets the milk from the refrigerator. I bet old Miss Hawkins gave her orders before I got here to not let me drink out of her "good glasses."

"Come on, honey. I'll carry your milk if you can carry your cake. Can you manage?"

"Yes, m'am."

"Just follow me, then."

Miss Trula carries my milk, and I follow with the paper plate with my cake on it. I put it on top of my book, like it's a serving tray. We head out a side door onto the big, wide porch. We turn left as we come out the door and walk toward two big, white wicker rockers that have cushions tied to them, for you to sit on. There's even a little white wicker table between the two chairs where Miss Trula sits my glass of milk. I follow suit and put my cake there, too. I sit down and place my book beside me on the rocker.

"Now, just make yourself comfortable here in this rockin' chair, Miss Emmy. You come and get me in the kitchen if you's to need anything. You hear?"

"Yes, m'am. Thank you for the cake and milk."

"You're mighty welcome, young lady."

She heads back toward the kitchen. I lean over and pick up my cake and start eating it. I lean back into the seat cushion and look across the field at the tall, white dairy barn. I don't think they keep dairy cows in it anymore. Seems like I heard Daddy say that Miss Hawkins sold them off, after her daddy died.

Now, wait a minute. I just noticed something . . . if I'm real quiet . . . I turn my head and look around the side of my chair. Why, I'm looking through some fancy lace curtains right into Miss Hawkins's dining room. I can see everybody, just as plain as day, well, almost; and even better, the windows are all the way up! I can hear everybody, too; if I concentrate. Ha. Ha. Ha. Guess you didn't plan on this, Miss Witchy Poo Hawkins. I can hear most every word y'all are saying; now that I'm paying attention. Maybe this wasn't such a bad idea after all. It's even better than my hidey hole. I can hear you, and I can see you. Well, well, well. This day is starting to look up, after all.

Hmm. Let me see if I can figure out what's going on . . .

"Darlene, it really is so good to have you here today. I've missed our Thursday mornings together."

I think that's Mrs. Maiden talking. I believe if I scoot my chair to the right, just a smidgen, there. This way I don't even have to crane my neck, well, not too much. I smile to myself.

Nothing much is going on, though.

"Darlene, is Vernon in any pain?" Mrs. Frazier ask.

"Oh, no, Evelyn. He's not in any pain, now. The burns are pretty much healed. I do have to put cream on his face, it helps to protect the skin where it's still tender; but, he's not having any pain. Really, he's fine. We're fine . . . too." Momma's voice trails off.

Momma is telling the ladies what she keeps telling me. Wonder if they'll figure out it's not true? I have.

"Myrtle," Grandma starts talking to Miss Hawkins, "I's just tellin' Darlene on the way out here, that it's time that we start meetin' back up to her house. Reckon none of y'all ladies object to that, do ya'?"

"Esther, now, it's no trouble to have it here, and as y'all can see, I've got so much more room than Darlene."

"Myrtle, there's plenty of room down at Darlene's. There was before, and there is now."

"Well, now, what about Vernon? You know we can't all be down there at Darlene's house, a makin' noise, while there's a sick man in the house, Esther."

"Makin' noise, my foot, Myrtle! You just don't want to . . ."

"Stop it, you two! Mama, I told you not to start anything this morning!"

"Honey, I'm sorry." Grandma reaches over to pat Momma's shoulder.

"Miss Hawkins, if you want to meet here, it's okay."

Momma's voice starts quivering, "It's just, it's just . . ."

Oh great. She's starting to cry for good. When is this gonna stop? I'm so tired of sad stuff and tears. It didn't use to be this way.

"Darlene, honey, now don't cry. Me and your mama just get a' goin', and you know how she is. I don't want to upset your nerves now. Lord knows you've had your share of trouble this summer."

"Darlene," finally a voice of reason; Mrs. Maiden's talking now, "Darlene is there anything we can do to help you and Vernon out? I'm sure it's been hard on you this summer to deal with all that's happened. Maybe there's something we can do, like, take the kids more often, or, well, I'm sure that the meals have stopped coming. Do you need us to start cooking meals for you again?"

"Oh, yes, Darlene," Mrs. Frazier chimes in, "I'll fix up a week's worth of casseroles if you like. You can just put them in your freezer and all you'll have to do is heat them up."

"Thanks, Evelyn," Momma lifts her head and gets a napkin off the table to wipe her nose, "But I'm not sure casseroles can fix what's wrong with us. He's just so different these days, girls. Vernon used to be the sweetest, kindest, most gentle man . . . but that man's gone now, and I just don't know this one. He used to be so responsible, especially with the garage and taking care of us, but now . . . girls, it's just so hard to say this out loud, but I feel like I'm going to come apart if I don't tell somebody. Girls, if we don't do something about the garage, quick, it's going to be over for us. Vernon's not keeping the books. People are not paying their accounts on time. Mama, I hate for you to hear this here in front of everybody; but Jack was right, the day Vernon came home from the hospital. If he doesn't go back to work soon, we're going under, Mama. I don't want to lose what we've got . . . Vernon always worked so hard and we're certainly not rich, by a long shot; but we do all right, and we've always paid our bills on time and had some money left over. But you know, Vernon, he stayed on top of things, and now . . . well, now, he won't even hardly leave the bedroom to take a bath, much less go to the garage. Oh, girls, I don't know what I'm going to do. I don't want to become a charity case, but I'm afraid that's where we're headed."

Oh, my goodness. I can't believe my momma's telling all this stuff to the sewing circle. It's real quiet for a minute, until finally my grandma starts talking.

"Darlene, Claude and me figured all this had been a strain on y'alls pocketbook this summer, honey; but I didn't dream it was to this point."

"Well, it is, Mama. That's it in a nutshell. If Vernon don't get down there and start running his business, we're going to lose everything. He could apply for disability, that's what they told us at the hospital, shortly after the accident. He told them, no, in no uncertain terms. He said, then, he'd go back and run the garage; even made a joke about it. But things have changed. You've seen him, Mama. You know he's different, now."

The other women are just sitting there. It's like they're listening in on Momma and Grandma; just like me. Finally, Mrs. Maiden speaks up.

"Darlene, why don't you just hire someone to run the place? What about Junior McCall? He does a lot of work down there anyway, doesn't he?"

"He does, Sissy. He's been a real big help this summer; and he's a good man; but he just doesn't know enough to run the business end of things."

Momma just shakes her head, and then puts her face down in her hands, with her elbows resting on the table. I guess that's what they call "a look of resignation."

"What about . . . well, this may sound silly," Mrs. Frazier says in a real soft voice, "What about if you run the business, Darlene?"

Momma run the garage?! Boy, I thought grownups were supposed to know things. I'm only nine years old and I know my momma ain't going to run Daddy's garage! Why, does Mrs. Frazier think my momma's going to put on a pair of greasy coveralls and crawl up under somebody's car and fix it? I mean, I like Mrs. Frazier, but what does she think Momma can do down at the garage? I guess, maybe, Momma could pump gas, if she had to, but I don't think Daddy would like it if she did.

"Evelyn, that's, well, that's . . . oh, I wouldn't even know where to begin. Well, if I did, I wouldn't be so upset. Oh, that's just not even possible, Evelyn."

"Now, wait a minute, Darlene," Mrs. Maiden pipes up, "Don't necessarily throw out the suggestion. Why, there are lots of women starting their own businesses these days. You don't even have to start this one, it's already there. You just have to figure out how to run it. When I was in secretarial school, the library there had a bunch of subscriptions to business magazines. None of the other girls ever bothered to pick them up and read them, but a lot of times I did. There were articles in them about how women are beginning to realize more and more, that if they're going to get ahead in the business world, they need to own the companies, not just work for them."

"Oh, Sissy, I'm sure you're right, but I don't have any experience and those women you're talking about live in big cities and have college degrees. This is Ivy Creek. Y'all are real sweet to try and help, but, well, Mama, you tell them—things like that just don't happen here, right?"

Momma looks over at Grandma. Grandma hesitates a bit before answering.

"Darlene, when your daddy had the grocery store, I worked there, you know, on and off through the years. You even worked there, when you and Vernon was first married. Don't you think we learned a little something along the way?"

"Mama, there's a difference in running a cash register or stocking shelves and being responsible for the whole business. Why . . . I . . ."

"Darlene, before my own daddy died, I helped to take care of the business for this here whole big dairy farm. Why, we were one of the biggest operations in all of southwest Virginia and most of east Tennessee. I'm not saying I knew it all, but I had to know a lot. You might want to study on this a bit, youngun."

Miss Hawkins. Grandma. Have y'all lost your minds?

"Darlene," Mrs. Frazier begins again in her soft little voice, "It's just food for thought, and, maybe, who knows, maybe some of us could help you out. If I can be honest, too, I would love to have somewhere to go and help out, even a few hours a day. I've just been going stir crazy at the house, and, well, y'all know what happened with the baby and all, and how I've been, almost like Vernon in a way; a prisoner in my own house. So, what I'm saying, Darlene, I'll be glad to come and help you out. You don't even have to pay me. I'd consider it a favor to me."

I don't believe it. Not only have all the ladies lost their minds, Mrs. Frazier just made a speech. I didn't think she could talk for that long!

"Evelyn, I couldn't let you do that!"

I knew Momma wouldn't go along with them.

"Darlene, I'm your mother and I'm just goin' to say, I think you ought to start listening to these girls. Why, even Myrtle's encouraging you. Maybe you ought to think about this. Now, you know you did more than run the cash register and stock shelves at Creekside Grocery. I remember your daddy showing you how to do up the bank deposit and order inventory. There's a lot that you know that you're not giving yourself credit for. What's more, your daddy and Jack have both run businesses, and they neither one would want to see Vernon's business go belly up, for your sake, and the children's, as much as Vernon's."

"Darlene, I think you oughtta listen to your mother. Now you know this is an idey worth considering, if it's got your mama and me agreeing."

Well, la dee da. Miss Hawkins agreeing with Grandma. Betcha lightening strikes any minute! Now, they're all talking at once again, chattering away like me and Karen when we get excited. Momma's even looking up and smiling. Who would believe this? You just can't ever figure out what grownups are gonna do next.

Momma came and got me from the porch after she and the ladies finally settled down and got some sewing done on the lap quilts they were supposed to working on. They're also working on the stockings for all the old people at the nursing home that's gonna be put up for Christmas. She must have been doing some embroidery, because she had a long string of green embroidery thread still hanging around her neck. Now we're on the way home. She seems a little happier than she has been—I guess talking to the other women helped her to feel better. Sometimes, I tell Karen if something's bothering me; but you have to careful, even with your best friend, because she'll tease me if she thinks she can "get my goat." That's what Grandma calls it when somebody's teasing you.

"Darlene, I think you ought to consider what the girls was tellin' you. That Sissy, she's a smart girl; she could be a big help to you if you's to decide on doing something."

"Mama, I know you may be right. But, that's an awful big undertaking. I'm not saying I'm not going to do it—but, well, you know how Vernon is right now."

"I know, honey. It's your decision, but you should feel good that the girls were willin' to jump right in and help you try to figure it out."

"I am, Mama. Yes, I am. It does make me feel better to know I've got their support and understanding. You know, there is one thing that stuck in my mind that might help to work part of this out for me."

"What's that, honey?"

"Did you hear Sissy talking about those gas stations that Kenneth had seen up north? The ones where people pump their own gas and it's hooked up to some gizmo inside, so the cashier can tell how much they've pumped, without going outside to look."

"I did, Darlene. Well, I swanny, I never did hear of such a thing before, but that would be helpful if you's tryin' to run things by yourself."

"She said to call her later and give her the number to the gas distributorship's main office, that'd be the Gulf home office. I know Vernon's got that somewhere in his books down at the garage. She's going to call next week and check on that for us."

"Now, see, that's one thing you can do."

"I know, Mama. It's all just so overwhelming right now."

"It is, sweetie."

"Sissy also said she'd help me learn what I need on the bookkeeping, too, when she's not working over at Ed Hudson's insurance office. She is so nice, Mama. I feel like I can trust her and that she can help me out."

"Oh, honey. I know you can trust her. She's a good girl and you know your daddy will help you too. Why, he loves nothing better than to see a business up and running. You know that."

"I will, Mama. I'm going to talk to Jack, too. I just wonder . . . I wonder how Vernon's going to take all this?"

"Probably not very good," Grandma snorts, and then adds, "But, Darlene, I don't see as he's leaving you with many choices these days."

"You're right, Mama. He's not." Momma says, as we turn into the driveway and head up to the house.

Grandma was right. I can hear Daddy fussing, even though the bedroom door is closed. I know Momma thinks Timmy and me are asleep. I guess Timmy probably is; at least I hope he is. Daddy's not happy about the sewing circle's idea for Momma running the garage. I knew he wouldn't be—he's not happy about anything, anymore. I can hear their bedroom door opening now, and Momma hissing her words at Daddy in a fierce way.

"For once Vernon, I'm not going to keep the peace. I've always done that for you and everybody else, too. One of us has to do something and I guess it'll be me. I'm going to do what needs to be done before we go broke!"

The bedroom door slams, and I see the tail of Momma's robe fly past my door. She runs through the kitchen; and I hear the backdoor slam, too. I just lie real still and keep listening for her to come back in—but, she never does. I just listen to the silence, for a very long time . . . and then I fall asleep.

Chapter 7

I hate limp, soggy cornflakes for breakfast; but that's what we're having this morning, after Momma dragged us out of bed at the crack of dawn. She came into my bedroom early, while the sky was still gray, and told me to rise and shine. I rose, but I'm protesting the shining part; that's why I'm sitting here scowling at my cereal. If she was going to make us get up early, at least we could have had Cheerios; they don't get soggy. What's more, Momma knows orange juice makes my stomach hurt, first thing in the morning, but she poured me some anyway.

"Momma," Timmy whines, "Please, please, please, don't make me go stupid clothes shopping."

"I'm not, Timmy. Besides, that's tomorrow, not today, and it'll just be Emmybeth and me, girls only."

"Then why did you get us up so early, Momma?"

"I told you, Timmy. I've got lots to do today, and you and Emmybeth will have to come with me."

"Momma," I ask, "Just what is it that we're doing today?"

"Well, Emmy, it's just that I need to go over and talk with Grandma and Grandpop this morning, before Grandpop runs Grandma to town for her hair appointment. Then I need to go by the garage and talk to Papaw Jack. I've just got lots to do, Emmy."

"Okay."

Well, I guess she's got lots to do. That doesn't really tell me what, though. Sometimes I feel like Will Robinson on *Lost in Space*. I think I've landed in a different galaxy and my parents have turned into aliens.

"Hop to it, Emmybeth, and you, too, Timmy. We need to hit the road."

"Okay, Momma," I say as I take my bowl to the sink.

"Momma."

"What Timmy? Come on, now, hurry up."

"Well, Momma, if you are going shopping tomorrow, can I have blue "tenny" shoes this year?"

"We'll see, Timmy, now go on and get dressed."

Oh, brother. Timmy sure must not be worried about how things are going these days, if all he's thinking about is the color of his new "tenny" shoes. He doesn't even get it . . . I guess that makes him the lucky one.

"Come on in here, you little rascal. You too, Emmybeth."

Grandpop's face lights up when he sees us coming through the back door. Him and Grandma are still sitting at the breakfast table eating the last of their biscuits and gravy and drinking coffee. If Momma was going to get us up so early, why didn't she just let us eat breakfast down here? Their breakfast sure looks better than ours did.

"Darlene, honey, is everything okay this morning?" Grandma looks concerned.

"Mama, everything's just fine, really. I just wanted to come down and talk to you and Daddy before you took off this morning."

"Grandpop, Grandpop, come in the den with me. We'll play checkers."

"No, Timmy," Momma says before Grandpop can speak. "You go on into the den and see what you can find on TV. I need to talk to Grandpop."

"Momma," I speak up before she can send me with him, "May I stay in here and eat a jelly biscuit? I didn't eat much of my cereal and I'm getting a little bit hungry, now."

"Why sure you can, child. Darlene, I'll get the jelly. You just sit right down at the table, Emmybeth. Grandma can't have her little girl going around hungry. Darlene, would you like a cup of coffee?"

Grandma gets up from her chair. Timmy's long gone down the hallway toward the den.

"No coffee, Mama. I'm fine. Daddy, I need some help. Emmy, I guess it's okay for you to hear this, you will soon enough anyway."

Momma takes out a red, spiral composition notebook from her purse and gets a pen from the pocket on the side of her purse. She takes the top from the pen and lays it down beside the notebook. It looks like she's already been writing in the notebook; she has to turn several pages to get to a blank one. It's easy to see why she graduated fourth in her class from Ivy Creek High School. She must have been really good at taking notes.

"Well, Daddy, I guess Mama's already told you about what we talked about yesterday, with the ladies from the sewing circle. It seems to me, that someone's going to have to run Vernon's business, and I guess it's me. Last night I started writing down some of the things we talked about— Sissy Maiden, you know, Kenneth's wife, she's a real good bookkeeper and secretary. She's going to check on some things for me with the Gulf people and well, Daddy, I know you ran Creekside Grocery for so long, I just wanted to see what you had to say, or what you think I could do." Momma's voice trails away.

"Well . . . let me see. Darlene, running a business is a mighty big job. Don't you think maybe Vernon will get back to it soon? Couldn't you wait a few more weeks? Surely, Jack and Junior could make it til' then."

"Daddy, Vernon's not coming back. He's made that plain to me; more than once. Jack and Junior are doing okay, but Jack keeps saying that with cold weather coming on he won't be at the garage as much. Daddy, you know how he goes on about the cold bothering his legs. I'm not saying it doesn't, but he's pretty set in his ways; you know that for a fact. He's always stuck close to home in the wintertime."

"Yeah, that's true. Well, honey, I guess you may have a point. But, now, Jack's gonna have to be the one that helps you with the garage end of things. I'm a grocer man, you know that."

"I know, Daddy, but running a business, is running a business, regardless of what you sell. You've always told me that— now it looks like I'm going to have to test it."

"Darlene, me and your Daddy was talkin' last night, that maybe you orta' think about puttin' in some groceries down there." Grandma speaks up.

"You know, Darlene, I think that might not be a bad idey," Grandpop straightens up in his chair and pushes back his breakfast plate. "You know that since I retired, we ain't had no grocery store here in Ivy Creek. It might even build up into a purty good business. Then, that way if you ever lost Junior as your mechanic, you'd have the grocery trade as a backup. Even though it's not more than two or three miles to drive over to Apple Grove if you want to pick up a loaf of bread or get a gallon of milk, it'd still be better if you could get it right here in Ivy Creek. You know I had a pretty good business for a lot of years."

"That's right, honey." Grandma says, "You could just keep the incidentals. You know people are going to drive over to the Giant supermarket to do their weekly grocery shopping, but it sure would be nice to have a place to pick up your day to day needs, right here in Ivy Creek."

"You know, that eases my mind, y'all," Momma says as she writes in her notebook, "I don't know much about the garage, but I'd feel comfortable running a little grocery store. Evelyn and Miss Hawkins said they'd help out. They could run the cash register and watch things for me if I had to be somewhere else. This almost feels like something I could do."

"Of course, you can, Darlene," Grandma looks over at me and winks, "Why, even Emmybeth can help you out, right honey?"

"I guess, Grandma."

Geez. I know she means well, but I'm not sure of anything anymore.

"Darlene, if you want me to, I could call up some of my suppliers. I know a lot of them old boys that are still runnin' routes. They just don't come out this way anymore, since there's no need for them."

"Oh, Daddy, if you would, that sure would help me out. I need to go down and talk to Jack and let him know what's going on—I guess, Daddy, if you can come down on Monday, when the garage is closed for Labor Day, you and I could look around the office and see what needs to be done, to convert it into a little store area. Would you do that?"

"Why, don't see no reason that I can't."

"Lord, Claude, look at the time. Darlene, I've got to go get ready. You know I have to be at Char-Lita's at nine. I can't believe you're giving up your hair appointment today, Darlene, you must mean business. Charlene called me last night after supper and told me that you said I could come in during your appointment, instead of my usual one o'clock."

"I know, Mama. I've just got things to do today that are more important. Thank you, Daddy. Emmybeth, you run and get Timmy and tell him it's time to go."

I head out to the den. There's one thing I do know for sure, now. An alien has possessed my momma. She doesn't even miss her hair appointment if me or Timmy is sick. If one of us is sick, she gets Grandma to watch us while she goes and gets a shampoo and set. Now, I know the world is coming to an end!

It really is pretty outside today. I can't believe this is the last Friday before I have to go back to school. It just seems like summertime has gone by too fast this year. Plus, we didn't even get to do a lot of the things we normally do; like take my daddy's old tent and go up to Roan Mountain to go camping or go down to Gatlinburg and stay at Oglethorpe's motel. I liked it when we went last summer, and Daddy taught me to dive into the deep end of the pool. We're on our way now over to the garage to see Papaw Jack. I wonder what Momma's going to write down in her composition notebook after she talks to him.

"Momma, can Glenn come over to play this afternoon?"

"Probably not today, Timmy," Momma says as we pull into the garage parking lot. "Come on you two, let's go see Papaw Jack."

We get out of the car when Momma gets it parked and head into the front door of the office. It's weird coming here and not seeing Daddy.

"Papaw Jack," Timmy says as he runs through the front door.

"Well, looka here, Junior. It's Darlene and the grandyoungguns. Darlene, everything all right up to the house? Vernon okay?"

"Oh, yes, Jack. We're all doing just fine. I've just come down to talk to you about something."

"Papaw, can I go out to the garage? Please, please."

"Now, Timmy, you know me and your daddy don't let you out there. There's too much dangerous things out there for a little feller."

"Darlene, I'll take Timmy out there if he's a wantin' to go. I'll watch him good."

"Thank you, Junior. Yes, it would be helpful," Momma says as she puts down her pocketbook. "Timmy's probably tired of following me around this morning, Junior."

"Okay, come on with me, Timmy, but now, you hold my hand and stay with me."

"Yes sir, Mr. McCall," Timmy says with a salute.

Junior laughs as they head out through the door into the garage.

"Emmybeth, you want you a peppermint this morning? Let me see. I believe I got one right here in my pocket." Papaw Jack reaches into the pocket of his work shirt and pulls out a Starlight peppermint, just like always.

"Thanks, Papaw."

"Darlene, what have you got on your mind this morning, that's got you down here so early?" Papaw Jack says as he sits down on his bench. He's always kept a bench here by the front window as long as I can remember. Daddy calls it "Pappy's Perch." He used to grin when he called it that, and Momma would tell him not to be disrespectful to his daddy. Daddy would say it wasn't disrespect, he was just funnin'.

"Well, Jack. I've come up with a plan. Now, you know, better than anyone that something has got to be done about this business. This is our livelihood, and Vernon doesn't seem to be too interested in taking care of it, anymore. So, I got to talking with some of the girls, you know, from my sewing circle; and well, Jack, I think I'm gonna step in and oversee this place. Maybe Vernon will get on his feet in a few months, we'll see; but, in the meantime, I intend to see that we don't go under. I don't expect you to believe right off that I can do it, Jack; but I'm going to give it my best try. Daddy's going to help me get this front fixed up with some groceries to sell, and the girls from the circle are going to take shifts helping me . . . and . . ." Momma's talking really fast, and then she seems to run out of steam.

"Darlene, well, I ain't never thought of you even wantin' to do anything like that; and Lord knows I never thought a young girl like yourself would consider it—but, now, let's think about this." Papaw Jack pulls off his cap and slicks back his hair before he puts the cap back on again.

"Jack, I know you may think I can't do this, but I don't see as I've got much choice."

"Darlene, I didn't say that—not t'all. You know, I've been afraid of what was gonna happen to this place. You know I don't get down here much in the winter; and like I told you before, Junior's a good boy, just ain't got no head for business; so, something has to be done. If you're the one that's willin' to take the bull by the horns, I don't see that I've got much cause to say anything against you. I'll do what I can to help you 'til cold weather, and then we'll just see what happens. Your daddy's a fine man; he'll be a big help to you. Them women will help you too. I'll tell you now, Darlene, this business belongs to Vernon and you. He bought it from me years ago, fair and square. So, as the sayin' goes, I don't have no dog in this race. If Vernon ain't gonna do nothing, then you gotta do something. Maybe this'll work."

My world just gets crazier every day. I never thought Papaw Jack would agree with Momma on this; but I guess I was wrong.

"Jack," Momma bends down and hugs him, "Thank you. I won't let you down."

"Darlene, you don't have to worry 'bout that—you just do what you have to. I'll help out as best I can. How's Vernon taking this?"

"Well, Jack, I . . . I guess as well as he can right now."

"That's pretty much what I figured. Now tell me what you and your daddy's come up with."

"Okay," Momma pulls out her notebook again and crouches down beside his bench to show Papaw Jack what she's written down so far. It's so hard for me to imagine my momma coming down here to the garage to work every day; that's Daddy's job. I don't know hardly any mommas who work; except some of the teachers at the school who are married and have children; but they're home with their kids after school and during summer vacation. I wonder what me and Timmy will do while momma's working here?

"Excuse me, Momma, Papaw Jack," I say so I won't get fussed at for interrupting, "Where's me and Timmy supposed to be while you're here?"

"Well, Emmy, I hadn't really thought that far ahead, but, your daddy's at home now, so I guess I'll just drop Timmy off with him, and you can ride the bus home like always," Momma says and starts to turn back to Papaw Jack.

"But Momma, Daddy never even comes out of his room anymore."

"Emmybeth!"

"It's true, Momma; and you know it's true. Can't I come here after school? Please!" I hate to be mean about my daddy, but I can't stand the thoughts of being at home with him all holed up in that dark room.

"Emmy, please don't be difficult," Momma says.

"Momma, please. You know how he is. Can't I get off the bus here?"

"Darlene," Papaw Jack starts to talk, "The youngun's gotta point. The school bus comes right by here. She could just git off the bus and stay 'til quittin' time. Emmy's a good girl, she won't git in the way. Will ya', Emmybeth?"

Thank you, Papaw Jack. I smile at him and nod my head.

"Well, I guess you're right. Maybe Mama and Daddy could watch Timmy of the afternoon and Emmybeth could stay here with me." Momma sighs heavily.

"I'll be good, Momma. I promise. I'll even help you with the customers, or sweep the floor, or . . ."

"Or sit in the back and do your homework, young lady." Momma says firmly and then even she begins to smile.

"Okay, okay. I guess I could do that, too."

"Now, Jack, let's see," Momma says going back to talking with Papaw, "Oh, yeah, I need to get that number for the Gulf corporation's home office. Sissy Maiden said Kenneth saw a self-service station up north, not too long ago. We thought maybe we could do that here. It would be one less thing to have to fool with, to not have to pump the gasoline."

"Well, I declare, I ain't never heered of such a thang. What'll they think of next?"

Papaw Jack and Momma go back to looking at momma's notebook and talking about her plans. Shoot! Sometimes I just hate that stupid battery that blew up in Daddy's face. I know that's silly to hate a battery; but it's the thing that made my daddy blind and I just hate it. I really do. It made everything different in my life, and I don't think it's ever gonna be the way it used to be. Stupid battery!

We're going to the Sears store in Johnson City. I love it when me and Momma can just be by ourselves; like today, we're finally gonna go clothes shopping for school. I just love to go in the girl's department there. They've got the neatest clothes. I even saw a shirt there one time, just like one Jan Brady wore on *The Brady Bunch* show. Momma said I could pick out three outfits today and a new pair of shoes. We also have to get some tennis shoes for Timmy, and a couple of new pairs of shorts and shirts for him; since he'll be going to kindergarten this year. He told Momma four times this morning to make sure his new "tenny" shoes are blue. He can be such a pain, sometimes.

"Emmybeth, do you know what sort of clothes you want for school this year? I can't believe you're going to be in fourth grade. Why, it seems like it was only yesterday that you were at Apple Grove kindergarten. I guess I don't have any babies left anymore, just big kids."

"Oh, Momma, Timmy will always be a big baby." Oops! I can't believe that just came out of my mouth.

"Emmybeth," Momma chuckles a little bit, "You're as bad as Grandma sometimes, saying the first thing that comes into your mind."

Wonders never cease! I was sure I would get busted on that —guess Momma's in a better mood today than she has been.

"Now, Emmy, you know you love your little brother. You need to stick together, you two. When you're older, it'll be nice to have a brother to lean on."

"Do you lean on Uncle Earl, Momma?" I ask.

"Well, that's a bit complicated, Emmy. He lives away, and Claudetta and Etta Jean live even farther away, plus they're a lot older than me. So, I guess to answer your question, I lean on them as much as I can, considering the distance. You know they've all been good to call since your daddy got hurt. So, that helps a little, to talk to them."

"Momma, do you think Daddy will ever come out of his room and start getting out again, like, you know, going down to the garage and stuff?"

"Emmy, I can't answer that—I know that doesn't help you out a lot. I wish I did know. I promise everything will be okay again, soon. Keeping the garage open, and getting the grocery store up and running will help us a lot. Maybe when your daddy understands that he won't have to do it all on his own, well . . . maybe then he'll come around. I'm sorry sweetie pie. I know this has been hard on you. You've been good to watch Timmy, and help me with things around the house. I guess I probably haven't told you enough how much I appreciate that."

How come when Momma's so nice to me like this, my eyes fill up with tears and my nose starts to burn? I can't cry again!

"Emmy," Momma looks at me sideways from the driver's seat, "I mean it, it will get better; for all of us. I promise."

"I know, Momma," I can't even look at her right now or the tears will fall out of my eyes and onto my shirt.

"Look, Emmy," Momma exclaims, "Two chocolate shakes for a dollar at Big Kay's drive-in today. Want to come back here and have lunch after we shop?"

"Sure," I say, glad to change the subject.

"Okay, it's a date. We'll shop, and then come back out here for cheeseburgers and chocolate shakes."

"Here we are, Emmybeth." Momma says, a few minutes later, as we drive into the Sears parking lot. "Are you ready to shop?"

"Sure, Momma."

We get out of the car and head into the store. The girls' department is on the left as we go through the front doors. I skip ahead of Momma and start looking at all the pretty things.

"Emmy, let me see the tag in that shirt you've got on. It's a size eight. I think you should look in the size tens. You've grown a foot since last fall."

"Momma, not a foot! I'd be as tall as you then."

"You know I'm teasing, sweetie; but you have shot up quite a bit, even this summer. You're quite the young lady, now. Let's see, Emmybeth. Like I told you, we can pick out three outfits, and then you'll need some socks and shoes, as well. We'll look for those after we find your clothes."

"Momma. Look here. I love this purple pants suit. It's got a long vest and a tie at the neck. Remember, I saw one just like it in the Sears catalog. You said you liked it too."

"Let me take a look at the price tag, and the size. Okay, you have to try it on though. Let's see what else we can find."

"I like this dress, Momma . . . and how about that green pair of pants and the striped turtleneck."

"Okay, Emmy, let's go try them on."

We head to the dressing room and try on the outfits. I just love getting new things, but I'm worried that this year it's too much. I don't want Momma to know I saw her taking that money from Grandpop though. She would just die if she knew I had seen it.

"Momma, I really like all three of these outfits, but we don't have to get all of them. A lot of my old stuff still fits."

"I know, sweetie, and you'll be wearing some of the things from last year, but this is all right. Now, let's think. You know, Emmy, you might be . . . hmm, well, maybe not. Turn around here where I can see you."

"What, Momma?"

"Oh, I just thought we might want to get you a training bra, but we can probably wait on that."

"Momma!" I exclaim my face turning red.

"I said we can wait, Emmy. I declare. I'm sorry. I didn't mean to embarrass you."

Oh, good grief! I can't believe she brought that up. At least I don't have to get one yet. Thank you, Jesus. Joni

Hendricks, this girl in fourth grade last year, wore a training bra to school one day; and I saw a boy snap the straps on the playground. Joni went crying to the teacher, and I know the boy got a paddling for doing it. I could hear him getting three licks out in the hall. I would just hate to think some boy would be snapping my bra straps. It's just creepy, if you ask me. Glad I dodged that bullet.

"Emmy, hurry up and finish getting dressed. We need to pick up a couple of things for Timmy; then we'll get your shoes and Timmy's blue tennis shoes. Couldn't forget that, could we, even if we tried?"

"Yes, Momma. I'm dressed, now."

"Momma, since I am getting older, do you think I could have some saddle oxfords and knee socks this year? Karen said that's what she's getting."

"Why, sure, Emmybeth. I don't see why not. I guess you are way too big for Mary Janes and anklets. I'm glad you mentioned that—I hadn't even thought about that."

My momma can be pretty neat sometimes. I wish it was this way all the time. She seems so much happier today. Maybe things are looking up.

Momma and I finish our shopping and head back to the car. I can't wait to get to Big Kay's. Big Kay's drive-in is one of Momma's favorite places. I like it pretty good, too. She says that daddy and her use to come here when they were dating;

only back then, they used to show movies here, too. She says they would watch a movie, and then Daddy would pull the car over to the hamburger stand for a bite to eat. She said every time they came here, she ordered a chocolate milkshake. The drive-in movie part is closed now. It's all rundown and weeds are growing out of the speaker stands. I wish they would open it up again. I think it sounds fun to go see a movie outside; but even if it was open now, we wouldn't be able to go. Daddy wouldn't be able to see the movie.

"Okay, Emmy, still want a cheeseburger and a chocolate shake?" Momma asks as she guides the car into the space by the speaker. I love it when the voice comes over the speaker asking what we want to eat. I've always wondered who the voice belongs to; because it's never the person who brings us our food.

"That's what I want. Is that still what you're having Momma?"

"You bet!"

Momma places our order and soon a teenaged girl, blowing a bubble with her bubble gum, brings our food to the car. She asks Momma to roll up her window a bit, so she can balance the tray on it. Momma hands me my burger and shake and we sit in silence a few minutes while we eat our food.

"You know, Emmy, I think you will really enjoy the fourth grade this year. It's hard for me to believe you're already nine years old. It just seems like yesterday you were my itty-bitty baby girl. You fit so nicely in the crook of my arm. I rocked you for hours. I thought that time would go on forever, but it didn't. You grew and you're still growing."

"Well, of course, Momma," I laugh, "You wouldn't want to be changing my diaper, still; would you?"

"No," Momma laughs too, "I surely wouldn't want that—it's just that I thought things would stay relatively the same, for a long, long, time; but they didn't. I guess I'm beginning to see, that the only thing that stays the same in life, is change. You know what, little girl? Change really is the only constant thing in life."

"Momma, what in the world are you talking about?"

"Oh, sweetie, I probably shouldn't be talking like this in front of you. I'm just going on—I guess I just wish that someone had told me, when I was younger, that life would be so full of changes. Maybe, though, that's something you have to learn on your own. I probably wouldn't have believed it anyway, even if someone had told me."

"Momma, I think I do understand, a little bit. I liked it better when Daddy wasn't blind. It's different now. I guess that's maybe something like you mean—it sure is a change."

Squeak. My straw makes a funny noise as I suck up the last of my milkshake.

"Emmybeth," Momma laughs, "Some things don't change. You always do that!"

"I know, Momma. See, not everything changes."

"Like how I love you and you love me."

"Yes, Momma. You love me and I love you."

Momma smiles at me, as I hand her the wrapper from my cheeseburger and my paper cup. She places all of our trash in the bag and puts it on the tray. She gets out of the car and takes it to the garbage can.

"Feel like heading home, Emmybeth?" Momma asks when she turns the key to start the car.

"Yes, Momma, I'm ready to get back and show Grandma my new school clothes."

"Then, let's go."

Momma pulls onto the highway and we head toward home. For the first time in a while, I'm looking forward to going there.

Chapter 8

It was quiet at our house this weekend, considering it was the last weekend before school starts. Yesterday was Labor Day. Last year, we went on a picnic with Grandma and Grandpop. This year we just stayed at the house. Momma made a whole lot more notes in her composition book and talked to Mrs. Maiden on the telephone a bunch of times. Daddy just stayed in his bedroom.

Momma's taking me to school this morning. She always does the first day of school so she can meet my teacher and know which classroom I'll be in. Timmy's coming along with us, because Momma has to have him over to Apple Grove Presbyterian Church by 9 o'clock—that's when kindergarten starts. He's all excited because he gets to take a bag lunch. It really doesn't take much to get him excited.

Momma's going on to the garage after she gets through taking me and Timmy to school this morning. I guess it's her first day, too. Grandpop and Papaw Jack are going to be helping her get things all changed around—so we'll have a garage and a grocery store. I guess Daddy will just sit at home alone today while everything is taking place. I wonder if he gets up and wanders around the house when we're not there. When we're home, Momma takes all his meals to him in the room. I know he goes to the bathroom, but it's right beside their bedroom.

"Emmybeth, next year, I'll be in your school."

"I know, Timmy."

"Can I be in your class?"

"No, Timmy. You'll be in first grade. I'll be in fifth. Don't you know anything?"

"I know you're a know-it-all."

"Timmy. Emmybeth. Stop it. We're already here, so pipe down. Come on Emmybeth. It's your first day as a fourth grader. Timmy, hold my hand while we walk through the parking lot."

Momma takes Timmy's hand as we make our way through the parking lot and up the steps of the school. We always have to go into the back entrance of the school because that's where the parking lot is. I don't know why they didn't make one in front; guess there's just not enough room there. The fourth-grade rooms are located all the way down the main hallway to the left. Mrs. Miller's room is on one side and Mrs. Brummit's room is on the other. I sure do hope I get Mrs. Miller. I can hardly wait to check the list outside her door.

"Here we are, Emmybeth."

"Momma, I want to check Mrs. Miller's list first. Oh, goody!" I clap my hands and then check for Karen's name. Oh, no! She's not in my class this year.

"Hi, Emmybeth."

I turn around and see Sammy Coleman standing behind me, with his mother and little sister.

"Hi, Sammy."

"Emmybeth, am I in Mrs. Miller's class?"

"Uh, I don't know," I can feel my face getting hot, "Let's look." I just hate myself. I always get flustered when Sammy talks to me.

"Emmy and Sammy, sitting in a tree . . ."

"Momma, make him stop!" I can feel my face turning bright red, now.

"Timmy Vernon Johnson! That's enough. Come on, Emmy. Let's go meet your teacher."

"Nice to see you, Darlene," Mrs. Coleman says to my momma, "Please let Vernon know I was asking about him."

Thank you, Jesus. I hope Sammy didn't see how much that embarrassed me. Momma leads the way into the classroom, and I resist the urge to pinch Timmy and let him know how I feel. I swear. He is such a little jerk.

"Mrs. Miller, how are you? I'm Darlene Johnson, and this is Emmybeth, and Timmy, her younger brother."

"Oh, of course. I remember Emmybeth. I've seen her here around the school, and her third-grade teacher told me I was lucky to get her in my class. Hi, Emmybeth. Hi, Timmy, nice to meet you. Emmybeth, you can look around for your seat. I've put a nametag on everyone's desk. We'll wear them today and tomorrow, until I get everyone's name, and then I'll staple them on the bulletin board. See, they're made in the shape of apples, to go on the tree."

"Yes, m'am. I see my desk right there."

"Okay, Emmybeth. Mrs. Miller, just so you know, week after next Emmybeth will need to start riding the school bus to our garage, instead of the house. Will you let Emmybeth know which bus she should take?"

"I would be happy to. Just send a note and remind me, okay?"

"I certainly will. Bye, Emmybeth. I'll see you at the house this afternoon."

"Bye, Momma."

Timmy turns around as he and Momma walk at of the room and makes a kissy face at me. He's so stupid. Sorry, Jesus. I know I'm not supposed to say that; but he is. I look around the room. Sammy's mother is talking to Mrs. Miller, now. Thank goodness his seat is a couple of rows over from mine.

Some of the other kids are coming in now. Man, I can't believe that's Calvin Bledsoe. He was the shortest kid in third grade. Now he's almost as tall as Mrs. Miller. Deanna Vickers got glasses. I'm glad I haven't had to do that. I guess I'm not the only one who's had changes over the summer; but I bet I'm the only one whose daddy got blind.

Mrs. Miller has turned out to be just like I thought she would. She's pretty and really sweet. She wears the nicest clothes and keeps a little bottle of Emeraude perfume in her desk drawer. When we come in from play period, she sprays a little bit on her wrist. I think that's just so glamorous. She helps us with our assignments, too. You just have to be sure and raise your hand before you speak. She did write Calvin Bledsoe's name on the board one day, for talking out of turn, but all in all, she's not mean like some of the other teachers.

Today's the first day I have to ride the school bus down to the garage instead of going home. Mrs. Miller handed me a piece of paper this morning with a number written on it, for the bus I'm supposed to ride. Luckily, Karen rides this bus, but so does Sammy Coleman. Just my luck he's sitting beside me right now. He keeps pulling at a string on his blue jean jacket. Karen's sitting right in front of us, so I'm trying to just keep looking at her, and ignore Sammy. Unfortunately, the garage is one of the last stops, and Karen keeps making goofy faces at me. Even if she's my best friend, she'd better not embarrass me. She should know better.

"Emmybeth," Sammy's voice squeaks a little bit when he says my name.

"What, Sammy?" I guess I'm going to have to turn my whole body around to look at him. I wish these stupid seats weren't so dang small.

"Well, how's your mother gonna run a garage? It's not like she can fix the cars or anything?"

"Sammy," Karen butts in before I can answer, "Everybody knows Mrs. Johnson's not gonna fix the cars. She's gonna run the grocery store part. Right, Emmybeth?"

"Yes, well . . ."

"And," Karen continues before I can finish, "My daddy's been down there a bunch of times the past two weeks and he thinks it's great. He's built all kinds of new shelves for the groceries. He says Emmybeth's mom is really getting everything in shape to make a nice little store for Ivy Creek."

Well, thank you, Karen and Mr. Mullins. Wonder what else everybody's got to say about my momma's business?

"It just don't seem right to me. You know, a woman running a garage; even if it has got a grocery store in it," Sammy says, more to Karen than me.

"Guess you just don't know much about women's liberation, Sammy Coleman," Karen replies.

Karen's really up on terms like that—I think her mama must be hoping Karen won't follow in her footsteps. She's all the time telling Karen about stuff like that. After all, Karen does have three little sisters and another sister or brother on the way in November. I guess her mama doesn't want Karen doing the same. Thank goodness, the bus is pulling up to the garage. Maybe I'll be saved from Sammy and Karen's debate.

"Sammy," I say as I stand up, "Number one, my momma's just running this place until Daddy can get better, and number two, well . . . just because you've never seen a woman run a garage, doesn't mean it's never happened before."

With that I manage to squeeze by him and start toward the front of the bus. Karen busts out laughing like a big ole' hyena. She kills me sometimes. It wasn't like what I said was that funny. I get to the front of the bus and tell the bus driver goodbye as I climb down the steps of the bus to the road.

"Emmybeth," Sammy hollers out the bus window, "Your mama gonna sell candy in the store?"

"I don't know, Sammy. I'll see and tell you tomorrow."

"Bye, Emmybeth," Karen yells out the window.

"Bye, y'all. See you tomorrow," I holler back as I head toward the door of the garage office. I walk across the gravel parking lot and wave to Junior who is standing in the doorway of the garage, smoking a cigarette.

"Hey, Emmybeth. How was school today?"

"Just fine, Junior. Is Momma inside?"

"She's in there with Timmy. You've not been here since she's got everything all fixed up in the office, have ya'? She's turned it into a regular grocery store. Your Grandpop's gonna be awful proud of her."

"I guess so. I'd better get inside," I say as I head through the door. I look around as soon as I go through the door of what we used to call "the office." It is unbelievable. I can't believe this is the same place it used to be. Momma's been telling me and Timmy every night when we eat dinner about what she's been doing down here; but it's different when you really see it. Why, Junior's right. It's not an office anymore. It's a real grocery store.

I look around the room and see that the old couch with the stuffing coming out is gone, and that the display case has been shined up. All of the windshield wiper blades and hoses that used to be in the display case have been moved over to the left-hand wall. There are shelves for some of the car parts, and others are hanging on the wall. There's a cash register on the display case and a stool behind it. I guess that's where Miss Hawkins or Mrs. Frazier will sit, during the time they tend to the store. There are some new shelves out in the middle of the floor. I guess they're the ones Karen's daddy built for Momma. The floor has been painted gray and it looks like someone was sweeping but didn't finish. There's a pile of sawdust swept up next to the shelves in the middle.

I make my way to the back of the room where the Pepsi-Cola and Coca-Cola coolers are lined up against the wall. There's even another cooler, and what looks like an ice-cream freezer. Man, Momma must have been busy to get all this stuff moved in here. It looks just like a real store. I guess it is. I know Grandpop has been helping her, but I didn't think it would look like this. I can't believe we own a store, now. I wonder where Momma has gone to though. She said she would be here. However, just as I think this, the door to the bathroom opens, and out walks Momma and Timmy.

"Hi, Emmybeth. Have you seen what we've been up to the past two weeks? I was just helping Timmy get washed up. He had a sucker a few minutes ago, and got more on him than inside his mouth!"

"Emmybeth," Timmy squeals, "Come here, and look in the candy case! It's neat. Momma says we each get to choose one. I choosed a grape Blow-pop! What are you gonna get? Can I have a bite? Huh, please?"

"Slow down, Timmy," Momma says getting him by the hand, "Give Emmy a chance to tell us about her day, and, by the way, no bites of anything for you, mister."

"Well, my day was okay, Momma. I get to ride the bus with Karen now. So, that's good. And, well, this all looks good. I didn't know it would look so much like a real store."

"It is a real store, Emmybeth. We've even got a new sign out front, under the old one. Did you see it?" Momma asks.

"No, I didn't."

"Well, come on. We'll show you. Won't we, Timmy?"

"Sure, come on, Emmy."

The three of us go out the door and Momma points to the garage sign that's mounted above the big garage doors. Sure enough, there it is. Right underneath the sign that says, "Johnson's Auto Repairs & Service Station," is a new, smaller sign that says, "Groceries." It has the words "Milk and Bread" on one side and "Soda Pop," on the other. I guess I just didn't see it before.

"Emmybeth, guess what else?" Timmy says as he's jumping up and down in the gravels.

"What?"

"Grandpop was here when Momma brought me here after kiddygarten, and he showed me how to make the cash register go, 'ding.' Want me to show you?"

"Okay," I say as we head back through the door.

"Come on, Emmybeth. Is it okay, Momma?"

"Yes, Timmy, but just one time, not a whole bunch of times," Momma says as we walk around to the register. "Okay, here we go.

"All right, Timmy. I think I can handle that."

"Okay, do it."

I push the button and sure enough, the cash register goes, 'ding.' Timmy jumps up and down and squeals, and I try not to roll my eyes too far back into my head. Momma laughs at him and tells him to go gather up his Matchbox cars and his coloring books to take back to the house. While Timmy is at the back of the store, getting his stuff together, Momma takes a key chain, shaped like a daisy, out of her pants pocket.

"Here, Emmybeth. This is for you. I thought you might like it. There was a nice man here today. His name is Mr. Robinson, and he owns the milk company that's going to supply our milk and ice cream here. He gave me this key chain, and I thought you want it."

"Thank you, Momma," I say as I examine the key chain. It's bright pink and has a brown center. There's gold letters in the middle that spell out Tri-Cities Dairies, Fall Branch, Tennessee. I'm not sure what I'll need it for, since I don't have any keys; but it is kind of cute. I know. Maybe I'll get one of those diaries that have a key for Christmas this year; then I can use it.

"Momma, may I pick out my candy, too?"

"Sure, Emmy, go ahead; but remember, it's not something we can do every day. Today's a treat."

"Okay," I say and walk to the front of the case to look and see what's in there. I really like Reese's Cups. I think that's what I'll choose. Actually, this is kind of fun. I walk around to the back of the display case and get my candy as Momma and Timmy come to the front of the store.

"Momma, when will Daddy be coming down to see everything?"

The words are out of my mouth before I realize exactly what I've said. My lip starts to quiver, and tears quickly fill my eyes as a sob escapes from my throat. I'm so stupid, just so stupid. How could I forget? Momma comes over to me and puts her arms around me. What's more, to my surprise, Timmy follows her lead, and puts his arms around my waist. He pats my back and keeps saying, "It'll be all right," just like Momma always says. We stand in our tight little circle for a few minutes when suddenly Momma pulls back and claps her hands together.

"I know just what we need," Momma exclaims as she starts walking toward the back cooler.

"The soda pop man left a whole case of Mountain Dew for us this morning. He said it was our complimentary gift for being a new account. Emmybeth, go in the bathroom and get us three paper cups. Timmy, you come here, too."

I go to the tiny little restroom at the back of the store, and get the cups for Momma, from the dispenser above the sink. I go back out to the cooler where she's opening a bottle of Mountain Dew. I can't believe this, soda pop and candy, both before supper. Maybe this is going to be a good thing for us—having a store, I mean.

"Okay, we're going to have a toast, just like the stars do in Hollywood when they make a big movie. We're going to toast the opening of Johnson's Grocery Store," Momma says as she holds her paper cup up in the air.

"Emmybeth," she says as she touches her cup to mine, "Timmy," she says and touches his paper cup, "To our success!"

Timmy begins to giggle like a wild man, although I have real doubts that he knows why. Momma and I laugh at his silliness, and my question about Daddy goes unanswered for the moment; but that's okay. Sometimes, you don't need an answer; just a hug, and a cup of Mountain Dew.

Momma's got everything ready for the grand opening at our grocery store today. It's hard to believe that we're really doing it. Daddy won't come, and Timmy's staying with Grandpop and Grandma, and coming over later in the morning. Daddy didn't even come out of the bedroom this morning and wish Momma good luck. I don't know why I expected him to—I guess I just thought he might try to do the right thing. I'm riding down to the store with Momma. It is way earlier than I usually get up on Saturday morning, but I was too excited to sleep anyway.

"Momma, do you think a lot of people will come in today? Do you think we'll make a lot of money?"

"Emmybeth," Momma chuckles lightly, "I don't know if we'll make any money or not. The important thing is though, that we speak to everybody who comes in, and treat them well. It's what Grandpop calls 'building your customer base.'"

"Customer base?" I exclaim, "What in the world is that?"

"Well, it's like this," Momma says, dropping her voice to sound like Grandpop, "Your customer base is the people who keep you in business. There the ones who stop on a regular basis, to pick up the groceries they need day-to-day. You want to 'keep 'em happy and keep 'em comin,' according to Grandpop, that is."

"Momma, you don't sound anything like Grandpop."

We both laugh as she pulls into the parking lot at our combination grocery store and garage. We get out of the car and head over to the door. Momma unlocks it and reaches around to turn the "Closed" sign to the side that tells everyone we're "Open" for business. She turns on the overhead fluorescent lights and goes back to flip the switch to turn on the light in the milk cooler. We both hang our coats on the hooks next to the bathroom door.

Momma and I head back to the front of the store, where she goes to the cash register. She takes a bank bag out of her purse and pulls out an envelope filled with enough bills to make change for the day. She keeps the rolls of quarters, dimes, nickels and pennies in a red metal lock box in a locked cabinet behind the display case. She gets all of the change counted out into the cash register and turns to me and smiles.

"See, Emmybeth, first order of business, out of the way. All we have to do now is wait on the customers."

"Okay, Momma. How will anybody know we're here?"

"Well, you saw our new sign the other day, and then Junior put a sign out there at the edge of the parking lot. See?" She says as she points out the front window. "Let's see, we've also told everyone at the sewing circle. Sissy Maiden made a poster and put it on the front door of Mr. Hudson's insurance agency. Plus, well, not to be mean or anything, but you know Miss Hawkins has told a lot of people." Momma says with a grin.

"Momma, do you think Daddy will ever come down here? I mean, is he ever going to come out of the bedroom or be like he used to be?"

"Emmybeth, it's just hard to know what your daddy is going to do these days. I guess he's doing the best he can. You're a big girl, and I can explain things to you that Timmy can't understand, but, it's like this—even though your daddy is a grownup, he's still trying to accept and understand why he's blind. Just because he's a grown man, doesn't mean he's not having to learn a lot of new stuff. He doesn't just know how to be blind. He'll have to learn. He's never been blind before; just like you've never had a blind daddy before. It's going to take all of us a long time to adjust; especially your daddy. If you can, just try to be patient a little bit longer. I think he'll come around, eventually."

Momma finishes with a sigh just about the time the bell above the door jingles, and in waddles Miss Hawkins.

"Miss Hawkins," Momma exclaims, "Why, you're our first customer! Isn't she Emmybeth? We were just sitting here waiting to see who would be first."

"Now, Darlene, you know I'm going to be a' helpin' you out too. So, I'm more than just a customer. Don't you reckon?"

"You sure are, Miss Hawkins. Let me show you around."

Momma slips by me to go around the counter and join Miss Hawkins. She takes her on a quick tour around the store. Of course, it's really not that big, so the tour is short. They stand by the shelves in the middle of the floor and Momma tells Miss Hawkins that the bottom two shelves are for a few canned goods and such. Grandpop told her just to try a few things and see how they sold.

"Darlene, I'm right proud of you, youngun. Looks like you've done this up right. Now, I'll just go around and pick up a few things, and you can ring me up. Are you gonna have your girl there runnin' the cash register?"

"Oh no, Miss Hawkins. Emmybeth just came with me today to keep me company on our first day. She'll be here in the afternoons, after school and all, but she's not running the register. Maybe she'll help me bag the groceries, right Emmybeth?"

"Sure, Momma. I can bag them just like they do at the Giant supermarket. I know you're not supposed to squish the bread or break the eggs."

"Emmybeth, you just got yourself promoted to head bagger!" Momma laughs at her own joke.

"Darlene, when would you like for me to come in, and help you out next week?" Miss Hawkins asks as she reaches for a loaf of bread.

"Well, let's see. Evelyn is going to come in the morning for a couple of hours, so I can take Timmy to kindergarten and run by the bank and such. If you could come in after lunch, so I can run and pick up Timmy at one o'clock and drop him at Mama's, it sure would help me out. He just goes to kindergarten, Monday through Thursday, so it's just a few hours a week that I need to have someone here. I really would appreciate it, ever so much. And of course, now, I'll pay you for your time."

"You'll do no such thing. Darlene, I don't need the money. I'm just glad to have somewhere to go."

Momma tries to say something, but Miss Hawkins holds up her hand.

"Darlene, I'm telling you. It gets lonely out there in that big old house with no one but Miss Trula to talk to; I guess you can see she's getting pretty old. To tell you the truth, I take more care of her than she does of me; not that she'd admit it. Anyways, just let me do this for you. If it gets to be too much, or if I get to feelin' like I need the pay, I'll tell you, Darlene."

Momma's eyes tear up just a bit and then she regains her composure.

"I sure do thank you, Miss Hawkins. Emmybeth, why don't you help Miss Hawkins get her groceries gathered up, and then you can bag them for her?"

"Yes, m'am," I say to Momma, and for once I almost don't mind helping Miss Hawkins. I guess she is nicer than I realized. Who knows? Maybe I'll even carry her groceries to her car for her.

The rest of the day goes by quickly. Mrs. Frazier and her husband came by, and her and momma talked about what she's gonna be doing to help out here at the store. Grandpop and Grandma brought Timmy down for a little bit. Mrs. Maiden came in by herself. Her husband is out on the road, most of the time now, she told Momma. She also told Momma that she had talked to the people at the Gulf headquarters about the self-service gas machines her husband saw up north. She said they told her they're just for the service stations in the big cities; but Momma said it doesn't matter. Junior is here most of the time, and he can pump the gas for anybody that needs it.

I've mostly just put people's groceries in bags for them. Everybody's been especially nice to me. Sometimes they ask about my daddy, sometimes not. I guess I wish for the most part that they didn't. I don't know what to tell them. It seems a little bit wrong to tell them that he just sits in his bedroom all day long; but I'm not supposed to lie either. Momma just smiles and says what she always does, that he's fine, and we're fine. I guess maybe that's best. After all she is a grownup, so I guess she knows best.

"Emmybeth, honey, are you ready to lock up and head home?" Momma asks.

"Sure, Momma, I'm ready."

"Come on, then. Let me just lock up, and I'll be ready to go, too."

I head out the door and Momma comes behind me. She turns the sign over to the side that says, "Closed," and locks the door. She takes my hand, and we walk over to the car. We get in and head toward home.

Chapter 9

Oh, I swear, my eyelids get so heavy when Preacher Cates starts talking. Sorry, Jesus. I hate that this always happens. It was freezing cold this morning when we got up. Momma said it was the first heavy frost of the season. Grandpop said it was time for everybody to "fire up their furnaces." I guess that's why they've got it so warm in the sanctuary this morning. Maybe that's why I'm sleepy; not because Preacher Cates is talking.

Even though I'm sleepy, I feel happy this morning. Daddy came out of his bedroom last night and sat at the dinner table with us last night. It's the first time he's done that since the day he got home from the hospital. He didn't eat anything. He said he wasn't hungry. So, he just sat there and drank a Coca-Cola. He held the bottle real tight the whole time. It's like he was scared he might not be able to find it again if he let go of it. Even though he said he wasn't hungry, I saw Momma take him a bowl of chili beans, and some saltine crackers while I was drying the dishes. Maybe he still doesn't want to try eating in front of us.

It sure felt good to have him at the table though. I'm almost getting used to seeing him in his dark glasses and walking with his white cane. He even talked to us a little bit, like he used to—he asked me and Timmy what we were gonna be for Halloween this year. Timmy's getting a Superman costume. I'm going as a gypsy. I'm wearing the crazy quilt skirt Momma is making for me out of scraps of old material, and I'm gonna tie one of Daddy's old neckties around my head, like a gypsy woman. Momma said she would even let me borrow some of her costume jewelry if I'm careful and don't lose it.

"Anyone have a praise or a sorrow this morning? Your church family will want to pray for you, either way. Yes, Ed Hudson, I see you have your hand raised. Please share with us, this morning, what's on your heart." Reverend Cates says as he gestures for Mr. Hudson to stand up.

"Thank you, Reverend Cates. As most of y'all know, my wife, Sue Ann, has been battling cancer for the past year or so. Well, now, her sisters and I are taking turns sitting with her, and all of y'all have been real kind to bring food and help with watching Tommy." Mr. Hudson pauses, and reaches down to pat Tommy's head before he continues. "Well, it's been a long, hard fight for Sue Ann, and it looks like the Lord is going to call her home, soon," Mr. Hudson's voice cracks just a bit, "Just pray for her, and pray for us. It hurts awful bad."

Mr. Hudson sits down real quick like and puts his arm around Tommy. Momma reaches over and squeezes my hand. I know Mrs. Hudson is very sick. I heard Mrs. Maiden telling Momma down at the store last week. She said Mr.

Hudson barely comes to the office now. She says on the days she works he doesn't come in at all. Poor Tommy. He's a sweet kid, just kind of shy. He's younger than me. I know how scared I was when Daddy got hurt. I don't want to think about what would happen if he died.

"Preacher Cates."

Oh, Lord. Sorry, Jesus. It's Miss Hawkins. I sure hope she don't say something to upset Mr. Hudson any more than he already is. He looks like he's gonna cry.

"Yes, Myrtle. Do you have a concern this morning?"

"Well, Preacher," she says as she stands up from her place in the choir loft, "It's like this, I don't want to be improper, seeing as we're in church; but I've got a praise I want to lift up to everybody. I think it's only fittin' that we recognize Ivy Creek's new grocer, Darlene Johnson."

Everybody turns and looks toward my momma.

"Now, I know this is a church service, but Darlene is doing such a good job down there. And, now, this does relate to church business—The Ivy Creek Sewing Circle is meeting at Johnson's Grocery on Thursday mornings at ten o'clock, just like we used to meet up to Darlene's house. We just set up a big ole' card table in the back, well, actually Junior McCall is kind enough to do that for us, and he brings in some folding chairs from the garage for us. We just go right about our sewing and quilting on the lap quilts for the old folks out at Sunny Meadows. Now, if any of y'all women want to join us, feel free to come. We'd love to have ya' and need any help or support you can supply. Thank you, Preacher Cates, for letting me say that."

"Well, thank you, Myrtle; that was quite a lot of information. You women of the congregation, take note. Let us pray."

Momma looks over at Mrs. Maiden and Mrs. Frazier and smiles before she bows her head. Grandma says, "Harrumph," and pokes Grandpop in the ribs. He just chuckles and winks at me. Grandma's still shaking her head even after we're supposed to be praying, and I hear her whisper something that sounds like, "Lord have mercy." Of course, I guess I should have my eyes closed, but sometimes I like to sneak a peek and see what everybody's doing while the preacher's praying. I figure if anybody sees me, then they're guilty of looking, too. Of course, I sure don't want Momma to catch me.

After the church service is over, all kinds of people start coming up to Momma and asking about Daddy, and how she likes running the grocery store. Momma smiles and is polite. Of course, I guess for the first time in a long time, she's not just putting on, when she says Daddy's doing a little bit better. After all, he did come out and eat with us last night. We get loaded up into Grandpop's car, and head toward home. Momma and Grandpop laugh when they talk about Miss Hawkins telling everyone about the store. Grandpop says it's free advertisement.

Grandma's still a little aggravated that Miss Hawkins made a big speech about the store, but Momma tells her she doesn't think Miss Hawkins meant any harm.

Timmy tells everybody about what he did in Sunday School this morning. I just sit back and listen. The only thing that's missing is my daddy, but at least he's still with us. One day soon Mrs. Hudson won't be here anymore, and Tommy won't have his mother. My daddy is still around, even if he stays in his bedroom most of the time. I guess things could be worse. Maybe that's what Momma means when she tells me and Timmy that we should be grateful to the Good Lord for what we have. Okay, I'm grateful that my daddy is still around; but I can't help but wish he would come out of his bedroom and act like he used to. I sure hope Jesus understands.

I am beginning to look forward to my afternoons and Saturdays at the store. Like right now, it's late afternoon on Halloween. The air is kinda cold outside, and it's real cozy sitting in here with Momma. Sometimes, when I come in here from the bus, and I'm cold, she'll let me pour myself a small cup of coffee from the percolator she keeps plugged up in the back. I put a lot of cream and sugar in it so it's almost bearable to drink. Mostly I just like to hold it until my hands warm up while I tell Momma about my day. Today all I can think about is going trick-or-treating when it gets dark.

I can't wait to wear my gypsy costume tonight. The crazy quilt skirt Momma sewed up for me, out of scraps of material, has a black ruffle on the bottom of it that swings when I walk. It's so neat, I just love it. I'm going to wear a red turtleneck with it and lots of beads to make me look like a real gypsy. Grandma gave me a whole bunch of her old costume jewelry from way back in the 1950's, so I won't have to borrow Momma's stuff. I've got one of Daddy's old neckties to use for a scarf around my head; and Momma said just this once, she's gonna let me paint my fingernails red, for costume purposes. I just have to take off the polish before we go to church on Sunday.

Timmy, the big dope, is all excited about his costume, too. He's going as Superman. He's so corny, he thinks he'll be able to fly with his cape on—I wish he could fly, right on out of Ivy Creek into outer space. Sorry, Jesus. I know I shouldn't pick on him, but he's just so silly, sometimes.

Momma says we'll close up a little bit early today, so we can get home and have some supper and get our costumes on. We're just having grilled cheese sandwiches and tomato soup tonight though since we're going trick-or-treating. I hope Daddy will come out and see our costumes. Well, I guess he won't be able to see us. I hate that I keep forgetting.

Always before he would take Timmy and me trick-or-treating, and Momma would stay home to give out the candy. It'll be different this year, with Momma going with us instead. I don't know what Daddy will do when the other kids come and knock at the door, but I'm sure not going to ask if he's going to answer it or not. I sure do hope no one gets mad and rolls our yard with toilet paper if he don't answer. Sometimes the big boys do that. They say they're just funnin', but I think it's kinda mean.

Oh, shoot! Here comes another customer in—I don't mean no harm, but I sure would like to get out of here. Wait a minute —it's Mrs. Maiden. Well, I like her. I guess it's okay if she's just going to stay a few minutes.

"Hi, Mrs. Maiden."

"Oh, uh, hi, Emmybeth. Is your mother here?"

"Yes, m'am. She's in the back."

Well, now that's weird. She looks like she's crying. I wonder what's wrong. It's unusual to see Mrs. Maiden's makeup messed up like it is today. Her makeup is always done just right. She reminds me of the girls in the Maybelline commercials on television. Mrs. Maiden always looks so pretty with her big, brown eyes and dark, curly hair. Her hair is cut in a shag hairdo just like in the poster that says, "Glamorous Hair," on the wall down at Char-Lita's beauty shop. She always wears nice jewelry, too. Like today, she's got a shiny, gold leaf pin on her jacket.

Oh, man. I bet Mrs. Hudson is dead; that's probably why Mrs. Maiden is so upset. I can't hear what she's saying to Momma, but she's pulling a Kleenex out of her coat pocket and dabbing at her eyes. Momma puts an arm around her, as they walk toward the front of the store.

"Well, um, Emmybeth, honey," Mrs. Maiden stops and clears her throat then starts again, "Are you ready for Halloween? What are you going to be this year?"

"Well, Mrs. Maiden," I say, not sure where to look when I'm speaking to her; it seems impolite to look her in the eye. She'll know that I know she's been crying.

"Momma made me a gypsy costume." I say quickly, and turn to look out the window, hoping maybe a car will go by.

"Oh, that sounds original, Emmybeth. I bet you'll look cute. I'm going to be taking Tommy Hudson around to trick-or-treat tonight, but I'll leave the porch light on at my house and some candy in a bowl for you and Timmy. Make sure your mother brings you by, honey."

"Okay, uh, thank you." I say, not quite sure where this conversation is going. Why would Tommy be going trick-or-treating when his mama is dead?

"Bye, Darlene and thanks! You're such a good friend." She says, giving my momma a quick hug. "Bye, Emmybeth."

"Good-bye, Mrs. Maiden."

"Momma," I say after Mrs. Maiden closes the door, "If Tommy's mother is dead, do you think it's okay that he goes trick-or-treating with Mrs. Maiden tonight?"

"Why, Emmybeth," Momma exclaims, "Whatever gave you that idea? Sue Ann is awfully sick, but she's not dead. Who told you that?"

"Well, no one said it, but if she didn't die, then why was Mrs. Maiden crying like that?"

"Oh, Emmybeth, honey, sometimes you just think too much. You know that? Nobody's dead. Sissy just has a lot to deal with right now. Sometimes, even grownups need a good cry." Momma says.

"Then, what's wrong, Momma?" I really want to know why Mrs. Maiden was crying.

"Emmybeth, didn't you ever hear that curiosity killed the cat?" Momma says, trying to change the subject.

"Whose cat, Momma?" I say with a grin.

"Emmybeth, I know one thing, if you want to go trick-or-treating this evening, you'd better gather up your things and get out to the car. I'm heading home."

"Okay," I say, knowing better than to disagree with my momma. I can't wait until I grow up. Maybe then, I'll get to hear all of the good stuff.

"Look at me, look at me. I'm dunking my grilled cheese into my tomato soup. It's yummy, Momma. Watch me, Emmybeth."

Oh, brother. Well, actually, oh, little brother. Watching Timmy dunk his sandwich into his soup is almost as much fun as watching him chew it with his mouth open.

"I see you, Timmy boy. You'd better be putting that sandwich inside your tummy, instead of into your soup, if you want to go trick-or-treating anytime soon," Momma says as she puts the final touches on my fingernail polish. I'm eating with the hand that's already finished. I can't wait to finish eating and get my costume on and head out the door.

"Momma, what's Daddy going to do tonight when the kids come by for their treats? I mean, like, uh, well is he gonna answer the door?"

"No, sweetie, Grandpop's going to come up here and hand out the candy; but maybe your daddy will come and sit in the living room with him. You never know these days," Momma says as she blows on the polish one last time.

"Okay, sweetie, head to your bedroom and get your costume on. Timmy, hurry up so we can wash your face and change into your Superman costume."

"I'm Superman, Momma. I'm gonna fly from house to house to get my candy tonight. I'll be over top of you and Emmybeth, up in the sky. Will you wave to me, Momma? I'll wave to you." Oh, brother.

"Sure will, Timmy. Now come on, let's go, you two."

Momma helps Timmy while I get dressed, and we're heading out the door just as Grandpop comes in. He makes a big fuss over Timmy, as usual, and tells me not to eat too much candy. Daddy never does come out of his room; but at least with Grandpop there watching the house and handing out the candy, nobody will roll our yard with toilet paper. It seems like even when we're having fun these days, I'm still worrying about my daddy. I wonder if that's how Mr. Hudson feels. You always know in the back of your mind something's wrong with your world—even if it's supposed to be the day everybody gives you candy, and you can eat as much as you want.

It's icy cold out tonight. I'm glad Momma made me wear tights under this skirt, but I may have to put my coat on too. Momma keeps asking me to, but I really want everyone to see my costume.

"Emmybeth!" Karen squeals my name as she approaches with her daddy and little sisters, "Hey, Emmybeth, you sure look neat in your gypsy costume. Hi, Mrs. Johnson. Hey there, Timmy."

"Hey, Karen. Your, uh, ghost costume is pretty neat, too," I say, even though I don't mean it. Karen's mom is not much in the sewing department; not like my momma.

"Hi, Karen. Hi there, Mr. Mullins. Look at all these scary little ghosts you've got with you." Momma says to Karen's dad. I guess since it's almost time for Mrs. Mullins to have the baby, she couldn't do much more than make ghost costumes out of old sheets. They all look a little dopey to me. Momma says sometimes you just keep your comments to yourself, so I just won't say anything about it.

"Hidee-do, Mrs. Johnson. Them shelves working out okay for you, down at the store?"

"They sure are. You do such fine work; and I sure do appreciate you sanding and staining them for me, too. How's your wife? Is she ready for that new baby?"

"Yes, m'am. Reckon she is. It'll probably be another little girl though, don't look like we're ever goin' to git no boy. That's all right, though. We're awful proud of these little girls."

"You should be," Momma says with a smile.

"Well, come on now, girls. Let's keep movin'; it's gittin' colder by the minute out 'chere. Good-night, Mrs. Johnson, Emmybeth, Timmy." Karen's daddy nods his head as he's walking away.

"Emmybeth," Karen whispers, "I saw your boyfriend, Sammy. He's dressed up like a spaceman, in case you don't recognize him."

"He's not my boyfriend, Karen Mullins!" I exclaim.

"Sure, he's not." Karen laughs as she takes off running after her daddy and her little sisters.

I swear. I do wish she would quit teasing me about Sammy Coleman. It's just plain embarrassing.

"Emmybeth, come on now. We'll swing by Sissy Maiden's house and then to Grandma and Grandpop's. I'm ready for some hot chocolate. What about you?"

"Yes, Momma."

Momma, Timmy and me walk down the road a little bit farther to the Maiden's house. Sure enough, the porch light is on, and there's some candy in a bowl sitting on the porch swing. Momma only lets us take one piece each. She says it's not fair to take too much in case some other children come by. We head back to the road and start walking toward Grandma's.

"Momma, why won't you tell me what was wrong with Mrs. Maiden? I'm old enough to know."

"Yeah, Momma, she's old enough to know." Timmy chimes in, even though nobody asked him. I'd like to tell him to shut up. Sorry, Jesus.

"Well, Emmy, it's just that some things are for children to know and some things aren't. Besides, Mrs. Maiden confided in me today, and you know what that means. When someone tells you something in confidence, you don't go around repeating it to everybody else—that's just the way it is. Besides, what are you doing worrying about what the grownups are saying? This is Halloween, it's the one night out of the year that you get candy everywhere you go and get to stay out after dark on a school night. Come on, Emmybeth. You're nine years old. Don't try to be a grownup too soon. Trust me. It'll come quicker than you know it!"

"Yeah, Emmybeth, quicker than you know it!"

We really should call Timmy, Echo-man. He's gotten into this habit of repeating what we all say. I really could just knock his block off, but I won't.

"Okay, Momma, if you say so." I agree, just because I know Momma's just not going to tell me what I want to know. Oh, well. It sure will be nice when school's out again, and I can listen in on the sewing circle. I never get to find out anything anymore.

"Come on, kids. Let's run. I'm chilled to the bone." Momma grabs both Timmy and me by the hand and we run toward Grandma and Grandpop's house. Come to think of it, hot chocolate sounds pretty good to me too.

Grandma greets us at the door as we yell out "trick-or-treat." She and Grandpop tell us to come on in and get warmed up.

"Daddy, did we have many kids up at the house?" Momma says as she takes off her coat and places it on the back of her chair. She starts rubbing her hands together to try to warm them. I know how she feels; it sure was cold out there tonight.

"Well, Darlene, about the same as we usually have down here. Vernon came out a little while and sat with me. Seems like he's a feelin' a bit better these days."

"Yes, he is, Daddy."

"Emmybeth, come on in here to the kitchen. Your momma and Timmy can sit with Grandpop and get warmed up. You can help me with the hot chocolate."

"Okay, Grandma." I say as we head toward the kitchen.

"Well, now, Emmybeth, tell me all about your adventures tonight. You sure do look mysterious in your gypsy get-up."

Grandma takes a pot from the cabinet and pours milk in it and sits it on the stove. She always heats up the milk and then stirs in the cocoa and sugar. When she pours it into our cups she always tops it with miniature marshmallows, and lots of them; that's the way me and Timmy like our hot chocolate.

"It was fun, Grandma. Of course, Timmy kept running ahead and flapping his cape all around. He really does think he's Superman, but, I had fun, too. We saw Karen and her daddy and little sisters. They all just had sheets with holes cut in them for eyes; they were ghosts. We went by Mrs. Maiden's house, too; but she wasn't there. You know, Grandma. Well, uh . . ."

Maybe I'd better not say anything about Mrs. Maiden coming into the store. I might get in trouble with Momma.

"What is it, Emmybeth? Somethin' weighin' on your mind?" Grandma can always tell.

"Mama," my momma says as she walks in the room. I swear, sometimes, I think she's got radar. She always knows when I'm about to open my mouth and get myself in trouble.

"Yes, Darlene. We're just in here talkin' about y'alls' adventures out trick-or-treatin' this evening. What 'cha need, honey?"

"I was just wondering if you needed any help?"

"Why, no, Darlene. I'm fixin' these two cups to take out to your daddy and Timmy. I guess you could pour you and Emmybeth some. Don't pour me none. I done been eatin' on the Halloween candy. I reckon I've had my fill of sweets tonight. I'll be right back, girls."

Grandma heads out to the living room with hot chocolate for Grandpop and Timmy. Momma pours us each a cup and hands me a little bowl with marshmallows in it to put in mine.

"Yum, this sure is good, isn't it, Emmy?"

"Yes, Momma, it sure is. Momma, do you reckon Mrs. Maiden had a fight with her husband? I's just thinking that maybe that's what she was crying about this afternoon at the store."

I know she's not gonna tell me, but it's worth a try. What's more, it could really be the reason Mrs. Maiden was crying and going on like she was.

"Emily Beth Johnson. I told you earlier, enough is enough. If Mrs. Maiden had wanted you to know why she was upset, she would have told you."

"Who's upset, Darlene? Is it Vernon?" Grandma says as she walks back in the kitchen. "I told Claude not to say nothin' to him about stayin' in the bedroom all the time. I swear, that man can put his foot in his mouth more'n anybody I know!"

"No, Mama. Daddy's fine, Vernon's not upset. Emmybeth's just got a big case of the noseys. You know how she loves to know what's going on—I told her today she's just like the curious cat. Although she doesn't believe me that curiosity really did kill the cat," Momma says, looking directly at me with her eyes blazing.

"Oh, Darlene, don't be jumpin' on my little girl. She's just concerned, not curious. Right, Emmybeth?" Grandma says with a wink.

"Well, I, just, I just wanted to know why Mrs. Maiden was crying so, at the store this afternoon."

"Darlene, what's wrong with Sissy? She not feelin' well?"

"I swear, Mama, now there you go. Y'all just need to leave me alone and stop worrying about Sissy's problems, too. I'm sure when she's ready for you to know she'll tell you both; probably call you on the phone. I declare! Emmybeth, finish up that hot chocolate and come on. You've both done worn me to a frazzle! It's time we're all getting to bed!"

"Well, Darlene, no need to make a speech!" Grandma says with a chuckle.

"Oh, Mama!" My momma gets up and heads toward the living room.

"Emmybeth, your momma's really got her tail feathers up, don't she?" Grandma laughs when she says it. I don't think she's mad or nothing.

"I don't know, Grandma. She just won't tell me what's going on—I never get to know anything. Everybody thinks I'm a child, like Timmy."

"Oh, sweet pea, don't you worry. You'll know more troubles than you want, sooner or later."

"Grandma, now you sound like Momma. You're supposed to be on my side!"

"Oh, Emmybeth," Grandma says as she comes around the table and places her arms around me, "Don't you know, I'm always on your side? Don't you ever forget it!" I smile and hug her back.

"I know, Grandma, but it doesn't make me not want to know why Mrs. Maiden was crying."

"Emmybeth," Grandmas says chuckling, "You're so cute, I could just squeeze you to death!"

Grandma laughs and hugs me even tighter. Whoever said curiosity killed the cat never had one of my grandma's hugs! I believe she just might very well squeeze me to death, but I doubt she'll be able to squeeze the curiosity out of me. I don't think anything could get rid of that!

Chapter 10

Stop. Lurch. Go. I think when I get to be a grownup that I will make it illegal to put kids on a school bus—especially one driven by Red. He's been a bus driver forever, but, I swear, I think his driving gets worse instead of better. He's kinda old, like maybe close to Grandpop's age. Wouldn't you think they'd make him retire, instead of letting him bump us kids along the road every day?

"Emmybeth, did you hear about Sissy and Kenneth Maiden? My mama says they're getting a divorce."

Karen's eyes get wide when she says the word "divorce."

"Karen, are you sure about that?"

I wonder if that's why Mrs. Maiden was crying at the store on Halloween. Oops! I'd better not tell Karen that, or Momma will have my hide.

"Emmybeth, I promise you I'm telling the truth. I heard my mama and daddy talking about it last night after they put us to bed. Sometimes, I can make out what they're saying in their bedroom, if I lay real still and my sisters are quiet."

Hmm. Maybe that's why Momma wouldn't tell me why Mrs. Maiden was upset. I sure do hate it if it's true. I've never

173

even known any divorced people, well, except the ones on the stories my grandma watches in the afternoon, but, even I know they're not real. "Well, uh, Karen, maybe we better not talk about this.

You know, my momma's all the time telling me to be more Christian-like in my heart and ways. I don't think gossiping is Christian-like."

"Like getting a divorce is, Emmybeth? It says in the Bible you're not supposed to divorce, it'll make you unclean."

Oh, no. I sure don't want Mrs. Maiden to be unclean; even though I'm not real sure I know what that means. It's not like people could take a bath in a bathtub when Jesus was alive. I think they washed in the river or something like that.

"Well, Karen, I like Mrs. Maiden. I don't think she'd do anything that would be sinning. She's nice and she's pretty and she's even got a degree from Steed Business College in Johnson City. My grandma said so."

"Well, I'm just telling you; that's what my mama and daddy were saying."

I don't want to hear this. I mean, when I thought Mrs. Maiden was crying over a fight with her husband that was okay, well, not okay for her; but it wasn't like this. A divorce is really bad. It makes me feel funny just to think about it.

"Karen," maybe I can think of something else to change the subject.

"What?"

"Uh, what do you think will happen to Tommy Hudson if his mama dies?"

Way to go, Emmybeth. Why not think of something worse than a divorce? Like death.

"Maybe his daddy will marry Mrs. Maiden," Karen replies, "After all, she won't be married anymore."

"Karen, that's terrible. I'm not talking about this anymore."

I turn and look out the bus window. At least my stop is coming up soon.

"Geez, Emmybeth. What are you getting so worked up about? It's not like it's your parents or anything."

"Karen, that's even worse. Don't be saying stuff like that. My parents aren't going to get a divorce and what's more, you don't know Mrs. Maiden is either. I just don't like you talking about Mrs. Maiden. She's my momma's friend. She's even in the sewing circle with my momma and my grandma. I like her. I don't think she'd do that."

"Touchy, touchy."

"Besides, it's my stop. I gotta get up, Karen."

I get up and scoot in front of Karen so I can walk down the aisle of the bus. Sammy Coleman looks up and smiles as I walk past his seat. I just look past him and keep walking toward the front. The bus slows to a stop, with a lurch, and Red opens the door.

"Good-bye, Emmybeth, have a good evening."

I nod my head toward Red and walk down the bus steps. I head straight across the parking lot toward the store. I don't even look back and wave at Karen, like I usually do. I swear. This really upsets me. I hope nobody's in the store, so I can talk to Momma about all this.

"Hey, Emmybeth."

"Hi, Junior."

Junior waves at me from the garage and goes back to looking at the engine he's working on.

The bell on the front door jingles as I step inside. I see Momma in the back and she motions for me to come to her.

"Hi, Emmybeth. Did you have a good day at school? Here, sit down on the stool and let me fix you something warm to drink."

Hmmm, that's unusual. Most of the time, I just fix my own coffee when I get here. Of course, usually Momma is busy with customers or giving her stock orders to the salesmen that come through.

"It was okay, Momma. Momma, Karen Mullins said . . ."

"Emmybeth, wait a minute, before you tell me about Karen, I have something to tell you. Now, this is kind of grown-up news, and I'm afraid it's pretty sad."

"Okay, Momma."

Oh, Lord. Sorry, Jesus. Maybe it is true. I bet she's going to tell me that Mrs. Maiden is getting a divorce.

"Emmybeth, Tommy Hudson's mother died earlier this afternoon. Sissy just called a few minutes ago to let me know. I know that Tommy is younger than you, but I know that you'll be sad for him. Just remember, Sue Ann is not suffering anymore—she was so sick, you know."

"Yes, Momma, I know."

Wow. I really do hate this for Tommy . . . and his daddy. I can't imagine what it would be like if your mother died. I wonder if Tommy was with her when she died; or if the ambulance came and got her and took her to the hospital.

"Emmybeth, honey, are you okay?"

Momma reaches out and touches my cheek. I look up and try to smile.

"It's just really sad, Momma. I feel bad for Tommy. He's an okay kid, just real, well, you know how he is; kinda shy and he doesn't talk much. Some of the boys make fun of him; they're not very nice to him sometimes. I feel really bad for him, especially now."

"I know, sweetie. We'll just have to do what we can to help him out now that he's lost his mama. His daddy's a good man, though. He'll take good care of Tommy and watch out for him. It's just going to be harder for him, without his wife around."

I sit for a minute while Momma's words sink in and think about what it would be like if I lost Momma. It makes me feel like crying, really hard.

"Momma," I say almost in a whisper, "Are we going to the funeral? Will we see Mrs. Hudson in her casket?"

"Well, I'm going, Emmybeth, and of course, Grandma and Grandpop. I don't know about your daddy, but, you don't have to go if you think it will bother you. You've just got to remember, Emmybeth, dying is as much a part of life, as being born and living and breathing. It's scary, because it's unknown; but it's natural because it's the next step after this world. It's worrisome, though, when someone as young as Mrs. Hudson dies. It seems like to us that it shouldn't be her time to die, but God knows better. He knew she was sick and suffering, and now she's not. She's an angel in Heaven, looking down on her precious little boy; and even though she won't be here with him physically, she will always be in his heart. I believe that, Emmybeth, I really do."

I know what Momma says is true, but I still feel bad for Tommy. It would be really scary to have to look into a casket and see your mother laying in it.

"Emmybeth, I've already talked to Grandma. She's baking a ham and making some green beans to take over to the Hudson's. I'm going to go home and bake a cake to go with it. We'll take the food on over there, before supper, in case any of the Hudson's relatives are there. If you want, you can go with us; or if not, you can either stay with your daddy or Grandpop. It's up to you, sweetheart."

"Okay, Momma."

Momma hands me the cup of coffee she's fixed for me. She goes back to the front of the store and starts straightening up the canned foods on the shelves down the aisle by the cash register. Wow. I guess I won't ask her anything about Mrs. Maiden, now. It wouldn't be right since Mrs. Hudson's dead. I do wonder, though, if what Karen said might happen; that Mrs. Maiden might marry Mr. Hudson now that his wife is dead. Oops. Sorry, Jesus. I guess thinking about gossip could be as bad as spreading it. I'd better get out my books and start on my homework; it just might keep me out of trouble and keep my mind off of Mrs. Hudson being dead.

It just doesn't seem fair. Even if she is in Heaven, Tommy's mother is never coming back. I guess you know what's best, Jesus . . . but I sure don't understand; and I bet Tommy doesn't either. Sorry, Jesus, but this time, I really don't.

Grandpop decided to go with Grandma and Momma over to the Hudson's house to take the food. Since I didn't want to go just yet to see Tommy, it means I'm stuck here at our house with Timmy and Daddy. Usually I like to go where everybody's gathered; but for some reason, it just seems too sad, with Tommy's mother being dead. Of course, I was a little bit put off staying here with Daddy, since he doesn't talk to us so much anymore. I guess it's just one of those times when I don't know where I want to be; I just hope Momma don't stay gone too long.

"Emmybeth, will you come sit with me while I color? I'm drawing a picture for Tommy. It's a picture of God and Jesus and his mama in Heaven. That's so he'll know what it looks like, where his mama is."

Timmy is sitting at the kitchen table with all his crayons scattered about and working hard on his picture. I guess it won't kill me this one time to sit with him while he's working. At least he's being quiet, and not being a pest like he usually is.

"Okay, Timmy, I'll sit here, too. I need to study my spelling words, anyway."

I pull out a chair and sit down beside him. I look at the words for this week's test in my spelling book and try to study them, but they just keep running together on the page. I really don't want to break my 100/A+ streak. I've had a perfect score on every spelling test this year, but it's hard to keep my mind on my spelling words and not think about Mrs. Hudson being dead. Timmy works hard at coloring his picture while I try to study.

"Emmybeth, do you think Tommy's mama can still see him, even though he can't see her no more?"

"I reckon, Timmy. Momma says that's what she believes. Now, be quiet. I'm trying to study my spelling words."

"Okay."

Timmy goes back to working on his picture and I turn back to my book.

I can't believe it. I hear Daddy coming down the hall. I wish it didn't make me feel funny to know my own daddy is coming in the room; but it does. He taps his cane as he comes down the hallway toward the kitchen.

"Emmybeth," Daddy says as he enters the room.

"Yes, Daddy. Uh, we're here. I mean, me and Timmy are sitting here at the table. Did you need something?" I ask.

"No, Emmy. I just thought I'd come out here and sit a spell with you and Timmy."

"Daddy, Daddy, I'm making a picture for Tommy, so he'll know what it looks like in Heaven. That's where his mommy went. Did you know that, Daddy?"

That's my brother. Never one to sit back and let the conversation begin. He always has to start it. Of course, maybe that's good. I don't know much of anything to say to my daddy these days.

"Yes, Timmy. I know that Tommy's mama died and I'm awful sad about it. Little boys need their mamas. I'm sorry he won't have his anymore. Well, at least not here with him."

Hmm. That's the most I've heard my daddy say in one sitting since the day he came home from the hospital.

"Daddy, do you want some Coca-Cola? I can pour you some if you like."

"No, Emmybeth, really, I'm fine. I just wanted to check on you two and see how you were doing. What are you working on, Emmybeth? Getting your homework done?"

"Yes, Daddy. I'm studying my spelling words. I've made a hundred on every test this year. I don't want to break my streak."

"That's real good, Emmybeth. I'm proud of you. I'll let you two get back to what you were doing. I just wanted to check on you."

"Okay, Daddy. I'll tell you all about what my picture of Heaven looks like when I finish it. Okay?"

"You bet, Timmy. You be sure to let me know."

"Well, uh, good-night, Daddy." I say, somewhat puzzled by what's happening.

"Good-night, Emmybeth."

Daddy gets up and finds his way back down the hallway toward his and Momma's bedroom. Man, wonders never cease. I wonder what happened to make him come out here and talk with us like that tonight. Maybe he's getting better. I mean, I know he'll never see again, but it sure would be nice if he would talk to us like he used to before the accident.

"Emmybeth."

"Yes, Timmy," I say with a sigh.

"Daddy looks funny with them glasses, but I still love him as good as ever."

"I know, Timmy. I do too."

I look back down at my spelling book on the page with the words I need to know for tomorrow's test. I just wish the tears in my eyes would clear up soon, so I could finish learning them.

Practically everybody in Ivy Creek must be here for Mrs. Hudson's funeral today. I came with Momma, Grandma and Grandpop. Timmy stayed home with Daddy. It was surprising to me though, that Daddy came out of the bedroom before we left. He told Momma not to worry about Timmy while she was gone, that they'd get along just fine. He said for her to take as long as she needed at the Hudson's house this afternoon after the service. He even told her to tell Mr. Hudson and Tommy how sorry he is about them losing Mrs. Hudson. It's weird. He's been out of his room more since Tommy's mother died than he has since the accident.

I looked at Mrs. Hudson when we got here. Momma says they'll close the casket once the service gets started. She just looked like she was asleep, but she's real pale and a lot skinnier than she used to be before she got sick. I could tell they had a wig on her. I whispered and asked Momma why they did that. She said it was because all of Mrs. Hudson's hair fell out from the cancer treatment.

"Mommy! I want my mommy!"

Oh, no. That's Tommy Hudson screaming. His daddy is holding him up to the casket to look in. Mrs. Maiden rushes up the aisle past us to get to Tommy and his dad. Grandma puts her arm around me and holds me close. She kisses the top of my head. Momma gets my hand and holds it tight in hers.

"Here, Tommy, come here. Ed, let me take him. I'll keep him in the Sunday School class until time to go to the cemetery."

Mrs. Maiden pries Tommy from his dad. Mr. Hudson sits down hard on the front pew and puts his head in his hands and sobs. Oh, this is just awful. This is worse than when Mrs. Frazier's baby died.

"Would you look at her? Can't even wait to get poor little Sue Ann in the ground before stepping into her place. Humph."

Grandma jerks her head around and looks Hazel Griffin square in the eye. Boy, Grandma's sure not glad to hear Hazel's two cents!

"Hazel, I think that's enough." Wow, I can't believe my grandma said that.

Momma just pats my hand and holds her finger to her lips. I know that means for me to stay quiet. Grandpop looks at Momma and winks. Momma just acts like she doesn't see him. Wow. Who knew that funerals could be like this?

Reverend Cates steps up into the pulpit and starts to talk.

"Friends, let's all bow our heads for a word of prayer."

Everyone bows their head. Well, except me. Sorry, Jesus, but I really want to see what's going to happen. Two men in black suits come forward and close the casket. Mr. Hudson still has his head in his hands and is crying really hard; sort of like my daddy did the day he came home from the hospital.

Preacher Cates goes on and on about what a good woman Mrs. Hudson was. He talks about how she directed Vacation Bible School every summer until she got sick. He even makes a point of telling Mr. Hudson about how he knows what a wonderful wife and mother she was and that she's gotten rid of her tired, sick body and is worshipping with the angels now.

I know all of that must be true. In fact, I'm sure it is. It just makes me sad to think about Tommy, back in the Sunday school classroom with Mrs. Maiden. I don't think he cares much where his mommy is today. He just knows she's not here and she's never coming back. I know Mrs. Hudson's with Jesus now, but I'm not sure that's gonna make Tommy feel any better. I'm not sure anything can make him feel better right now.

I lean into Grandma's arms and hold Momma's hand just a little bit tighter. I know nothing feels better than my momma's hugs when I get hurt, but maybe, Mrs. Maiden can make Tommy feel a little bit better. I sure hope so. He's a sweet kid. He didn't deserve to lose his mom. Nobody deserves that.

After the funeral service, Momma takes my hand as we head out of the church. I'm going with her straight to the Hudson's house, while Grandma and Grandpop go to the cemetery with the rest of the congregation. Mrs. Frazier is going to the Hudson's house too, to help Momma get things set up. I'm not sure what I'm supposed to do, but I'm sure Momma will figure out something. Not that I mind. It's sure been an awfully sad day, especially for Tommy Hudson.

I saw Mrs. Maiden bring Tommy from the Sunday School rooms and give him to his daddy as everybody was lining up to go to the cemetery. His eyes were all red, and his nose all runny. I couldn't stand it if it was my momma they were going to bury in the ground today. I wonder what will happen now with him and his daddy. I wonder who will cook their dinner, and clean their house, and do all the things mothers do.

Of course, since my daddy's been blind, and my momma has been working at the store, she doesn't do everything at the house that she used to do. I guess Tommy and Mr. Hudson will just have to do like Daddy, Timmy, and me, and learn to do some of that stuff themselves. At least my momma is still around though. Tommy's mom isn't just working at a store, she's gone for always.

"Emmybeth, what are you studying so hard on, honey?"

"Well, um, I don't really know. I'm, well, I guess I'm just wondering what's gonna happen to Tommy and his daddy, now. Do you know what they'll do for meals and somebody to clean their house and stuff like that?"

"Oh, goodness, Emmybeth, I don't really know. I'm sure Ed will handle it. For a while, people will probably keep sending food like they're doing today. I guess for the most part, eventually Ed and Tommy will learn to get along;

kind of like we all did Emmybeth, when your daddy had his accident. That's what life is all about. Just when you think you've got things figured out, you get handed another puzzle to solve. You just do the best you can do."

"Well, Momma, maybe I'm not supposed to feel this way, but I don't want to ever have to learn to do without you or Daddy. I'm not glad it was Tommy's momma instead, though. I know that might be breaking a commandment to wish it was him instead of me."

"Oh, honey. You're not breaking any commandments. Sweetie, you're just scared. So am I. When somebody so young dies, like Sue Ann, it just makes you realize how precious life is, and how it can be over in an instant. All we can do is just live every day as good as we can. That's all, Emmybeth. You can't control everything. And part of realizing that you can't control everything is just having faith, sweetheart. You just have to have faith that the Good Lord is watching over us."

I nod my head, even though Momma's eyes are on the road and not on me. I know she's right. I sure do hope that the Good Lord is watching over Tommy right now. I've got a feeling he's gonna need Him when they lower his mother's casket into the ground. *Please, Jesus, please,* I pray silently while I squeeze the tears behind my eyelids as we pull up in front of the Hudson's house.

Chapter 11

Today's the day I look forward to for most of the week; it's Saturday, and I'm helping Momma down at the store. Saturdays are different than the other days of the week when I get off the school bus at the store. On those afternoons I just get a snack and for the most part, work on my homework while I wait for Momma to finish up and close for the day. On Saturdays, I get to help her for real, by bagging up the groceries. I hope it helps Momma. She's tired a lot of the time lately. I guess running the store and taking care of the rest of us can make her tired, though.

"Momma, do you want me to go ahead and bag up the groceries we're gonna take home today? You know, the ones you wrote down on your list last night."

"Not right now, Emmybeth, we'll work on that later."

"Okay, Momma. Uh, Momma, I was just thinking."

Momma puts down the feather duster she's been using to dust off the shelves and walks over to the counter where I'm standing. She looks at me with a big smile on her face.

"Emmybeth, why is it every time you say that I know there's something coming I may not want to hear or be able to answer?" She chuckles as she tells me this.

"Momma!" I protest a little bit, even though I know she's right. "I just want to tell you something I've been thinking about. Maybe I could get paid for working here on Saturdays. Now, I know this is for our family, and I'm really trying to do my part, but Momma, don't you think I could get a salary, you know, like a real working person?"

"Why, Emmybeth, of course! I don't know why I didn't think of that before! Of course, you deserve to get paid, sweetie. I declare! I don't know where my mind is these days. I'll pay you starting today. How about two dollars for every Saturday you work? How does that sound?"

"Well, I guess that's okay. I was gonna say a dollar, but two is even better."

"You're right, Emmybeth," Momma says laughing, "Two dollars is better than one. You drive a hard bargain, but I'll stick to my end of it. Two dollars it is!"

"Thanks, Momma." Gee, that wasn't as hard as I thought it would be. Sometimes I think I make things harder than they have to be.

Jing-a-ling. The front door opens. Momma had Junior put up a bell over the door so it would ring when people come in the store. She said it would always let her know when customers were in the store, in case she was in the back and couldn't see them come in.

"There's that Emmybeth, at her station, working this morning! How's my grandyoungun' this fine Saturday morning?"

"I'm okay, Papaw Jack."

"Well, hello, Jack. What are you doing out this morning? You usually don't get down this way, especially now since the weather's turned off cold. Would you like to come to the back so I can fix you some coffee and you can sit by the heater?"

"No, no, Darlene. I's jest waitin' to meet someone here this mornin'. Well, you see, it's like this . . ."

Jing-a-ling.

Oh, Lord. I can't believe it. Here comes Miss Hawkins busting in this morning. Wonder whose business she wants to mess in? Oops. Sorry, Jesus. I know that's not kind of me, but it's true.

"Well, Darlene, uh, Emmybeth. Well, hi, uh, Jack, how are you this morning?"

"Well, hidee do, there, Myrtle. You're a' lookin' mighty pert this fine day."

"Oh, Jack," Miss Hawkins says and starts to giggle, just like a girl.

I don't know what's going on, but I think if Miss Hawkins giggles again, I'll probably laugh out loud.

"Miss Hawkins, I was just offering to get some coffee for Jack while he waits here, would you like some too?"

"Uh, well, no, Darlene, thank you though. You see, well, I'm the one Jack is waiting for—he's gonna follow me up to the house and ah, well, you see . . ."

"Ah, shucks, Darlene, I's jest gonna go up to Myrtle's, I mean, Miss Hawkin's place, and check about some wiring she thinks needs fixin'. You know her hired man's jest not the best on wirin' and she thought I might know what to do. We'll jest be scootin' along. Bye, Darlene, bye-bye Emmybeth."

"Bye, Papaw Jack," I say as Momma and me watch them go out the door and get in their cars.

"Momma, why was Papaw Jack acting all funny like that?"

"Emmybeth, honey, that's a real good question. I'm not sure I know the answer to that one. We'll just see."

"Miss Hawkins was giggling. Did you hear her, Momma?"

"Yes, I did Emmybeth, yes, I did. Well, honey, whatever it is, I'm sure it's not any of our concern."

"Momma, that's what you always say; just like you did about Mrs. Maiden crying in here on Halloween." Oops. I'll probably get it now. Momma don't like me gossiping.

"All right, Emmybeth. You know, I probably should tell you about Mrs. Maiden. You're a big enough girl, and you're probably going to hear it anyway. I'd rather you hear the truth from me."

"What do you mean?" I can't believe my ears. Momma is gonna tell me something that just a few weeks ago she told me was gossip. Wow.

"Okay, well, let's see the best way to tell you this. You see, Sissy and her husband, Kenneth, are not going to be married anymore. They're getting a divorce. Now, you know that's not something I would ordinarily be in favor of, but, let's just say that sometimes it can't be helped. Sissy tried hard to be a good wife to Kenneth. She's a good woman, a real good Christian girl. She's awfully upset about this, so I don't want you saying anything about this to anybody. Some people will gossip, and we can't stop them, but we don't have to give them any information they might twist around and use to hurt Sissy. Okay, Emmybeth? I want your word on this."

"I promise, Momma. I like Mrs. Maiden. She's so pretty, and she was so nice to me the day Daddy got hurt. Why, she drove me all the way to Johnson City and wouldn't even take my money. I offered to give her money for her gas."

"Oh, Emmybeth, you're such a sweetheart. Mrs. Maiden wanted to do that for you. She's just that kind of person. She'd never taken your money, but that was polite of you to offer. Sissy just needs some time and our prayers. Maybe one day soon, all of this heartache will be behind her."

"I sure hope so, Momma."

Jing-a-ling. The door opens again, and a real customer comes in this time.

"Well, Emmybeth," Momma looks at me and grins, "I guess you'd better get to work and start earning your pay. I expect a lot of work out of you if I'm going to be paying you two bucks!"

"Yes, m'am." I salute to Momma as we greet our customer. Sometimes Momma surprises me. I guess maybe she really is noticing that I'm growing up—I sure hope so.

Seems like some days just drag on forever—today's one of those days for me. Momma got me up this morning and told me eat my Cheerios right quick like if I could, and then get Timmy fed and dressed. I got all that done, and now, I'm just trying to stay out of Momma's way. She's trying to get the Thanksgiving dinner on the table by noon. Nothing'll do except for Grandpop and Papaw Jack to eat right at twelve o'clock on the nose. Momma said so under her breath and I could have sworn she didn't sound too happy about it. She always does the Thanksgiving dinner, and Grandma does the Christmas dinner. So, I guess she tries to be a good sport about it, even though her turn comes first.

"Emmybeth, could you come in here to the kitchen please, and answer this phone? I declare, I'm never going to get this dinner finished if I have to stop and talk."

"Yes, Momma," I answer as I run toward the kitchen. I wonder who could be calling this morning. I figured all the people in Ivy Creek were doing the same thing my momma is doing this morning—you know stuffing turkeys and such.

"Hello. This is the Johnson residence."

"Emmybeth, Emmybeth, this is Karen."

She sure is excited this morning, of course, Karen is fairly excitable most of the time.

"Emmybeth, you're never gonna believe it! I've got a baby brother. Can you believe it finally happened? My mama says this is definitely the last baby she'll ever have. She can quit now that Daddy's got a boy."

"Well, um, Karen, that's good." What do you say when someone tells you something like that about their mother? Really, Karen gives out too much information.

"Yeah, I'm pretty excited about it, and so are my little sisters. Mama says Daddy's about to bust the buttons on his shirt, whatever that means. I just thought you'd wanna know. And, you know what else? They let all of us girls pick out his name. We named him John Michael. Do you like that, Emmybeth?"

"Sure, Karen. It's a great name. Is your mama coming home today?"

"No, she has to stay in the hospital a few more days. She told Daddy she didn't mind. She said it was like having a vacation with the nurses taking care of the baby and her getting to eat in bed. She says she's gonna stay as long as they let her."

I just bet she will. Even Momma says Karen's mom deserves a break—what with having to take care of all her children, and being pregnant all the time, too. And Momma never gossips!

"Well, Karen, I'm glad you've got a little brother. I just hope he don't turn out to be like Timmy." Oops. Sorry, Jesus.

"Oh, Emmybeth, you know you love Timmy—even when you try to act like you don't."

"I guess."

"Well, I guess I'd better go. My daddy's taking all of us to my aunt's house for Thanksgiving dinner. I just wanted to tell you. I'll see you at church on Sunday. Bye, Emmybeth."

"Bye, Karen."

"Momma, guess what?"

"What's that, Emmybeth?"

"Karen's mama had a baby boy last night. Karen and her sisters got to name him. His name is John Michael."

"Hmm, John Michael, that's a real pretty name. I like it."

"Yeah, and Karen says her mama says the best part is she doesn't have to have any more babies, now that Mr. Mullins has a boy."

"Oh, how funny," Momma laughs, "I guess anybody could understand why Mrs. Mullins would feel that way—

what with four little girls, and a baby boy all under the age of ten. I can't say as I blame her."

"Momma, do you think you'll ever have another baby?"

"Emmybeth," Momma stops stirring the big bowl of mashed potatoes she's been working on, and looks me right in the eye, "What on earth makes you ask that?"

"I don't know, just wondering I guess." Gee, I must have stepped into something again. I really didn't mean to; I really am just wondering.

"Well, would you like it if I did?"

"I don't know, it might be okay—as long as it was a girl and not another boy, like Timmy!" Oops. Sorry, Jesus. Again.

"I swear, Emmybeth. You are your grandma's girl for sure. I tell you what Emmybeth, if it happens, you'll be one of the first people I tell," Momma says, and then laughs the strangest laugh. I just cannot figure out grownups. They laugh when there's nothing funny, and don't when there is. I don't think I'll ever figure them out.

I'm supposed to be asleep but I'm having a hard time getting there, tonight. I think I must have drunk too much Coca-Cola with my Thanksgiving dinner. Maybe that's why Momma told me to slow down on drinking so much; even though it was a special occasion, and she let Timmy and me have soda pop with our dinner.

I really don't mind being awake, though. I'm beginning to like our house at nighttime again. I used to lay here in bed and listen to Momma and Daddy whisper to each other in their bed at night. It always made me feel so safe. You know, like I was in a special place that only our family could be in—but then it all changed.

After Daddy's accident, for the longest time I never heard them talking at night. Then, later on, sometimes I would hear them fussing, and it scared me. Momma and Daddy never fussed before he went blind; then it seemed like they fussed all the time; only they did it after me and Timmy were in bed. I guess they never thought one of us would hear them. Sometimes, Momma would cry. That really made me feel bad, and I would think about getting up and going to hug her or something, but I didn't want to get in trouble.

But, now, it's not like that so much. I haven't heard them fuss, or Momma cry, in a while now. I like it better, and I'm not so scared like I was before. I guess maybe we're all getting used to it. Daddy even came to the dinner table today. I didn't know what might happen, but it went okay. He even ate his food in front of us, and didn't get anything on his shirt, or spill his drink. I guess he's been practicing when we're not here during the day.

I hope things will go back to normal, as normal as it will ever get. I'm not sure I'll ever get used to the idea of my daddy being blind. I guess it's just like Momma says, we'll just get used to how things have changed and learn to live with it. Right now, I think I'll just try to sleep. Maybe all that Coca-Cola is starting to wear off.

Chapter 12

"Momma," I whisper as she's pinning the hem of my costume, "I want to be a good Mary in the Christmas play, but what if I drop Karen's little brother when I pick him up at the end of the scene at the manger? I mean, I'll just die if I drop the baby Jesus."

"Hold still, Emmybeth."

"But Momma, what if I drop John Michael, and his head gets squished or something awful happens? I'll go to prison."

"Oh, Emmybeth, that's not going to happen. You'll be fine."

I sure hope so. I'm not so sure I believe Momma, but I know better than to keep bothering her. Grandma says Momma's just plumb wore out from working at the store and trying to take care of Daddy, Timmy and me. She didn't actually say it to me, but I heard her tell Grandpop that, when I was at their house yesterday afternoon.

"Darlene, when you finish pinning up the hem on Emmybeth's costume, just hand it over here and I'll sew it up. All right?"

"Sure thing, Sissy. I guess we've got quite an assembly line going here."

"Yes, this is working out well. I've finished with the shepherds' costumes. Hazel is with the Reverend and Mrs. Cates in the sanctuary. I guess they're just about finished setting up the manger in front of the altar. I think as soon as I sew up Emmybeth's costume we can "call it a wrap" as they say in the theater," Mrs. Maiden says and laughs at her own joke.

"Okay, Sissy, here's Emmy's costume," Momma says as she pulls it over my head. Good thing I've got my clothes on under it. She just pulled it straight off without even checking. Honestly, she coulda asked if I was wearing anything under it.

"Emmybeth, you go get your coat, and we'll head on home. I bet Timmy's probably kicking up a fuss about taking a bath right about now. What do you think?"

"I think you're probably right, Momma. Goodnight, Mrs. Maiden," I say as I head to the coat rack at the front of the church.

"Goodnight, sweetie. See you tomorrow night for your big debut."

I head down the hallway and run smack dab into Hazel Griffin. She's not looking too happy. I wonder what's going on. "Emmybeth, where's yore mother at?"

"Hazel, I'm right here," Momma says as she comes down the hallway, "Is there a problem with the manger scene? Sissy said she thought y'all were finished with it. Is there something I can help you with?"

"I'll tell you what the problem is Darlene; that woman is the problem. I can't believe yore lettin' her sew up the costumes for the Christmas play. Why, she's got no business bein' involved with the most holy of holy stories."

"Hazel, keep your voice down. Emmybeth, you go on, now, get your coat and wait for me in the front of the church," Momma says with a look that means business.

I know I should obey my momma, but as I turn the corner to head out toward the front of the church, I realize Momma and Mrs. Griffin are still talking. If I walk real slow, I just might be able to catch the rest of their conversation. I know listening in is wrong, especially in the house of the Lord—but, sorry, Jesus, sometimes I just can't help myself. Besides, if I'm still walking toward the front of the church, it's not like I'm disobeying my mother. I can't help it if my ears are extra good, and I overhear what they're saying.

"Now, Hazel."

"Don't you 'now, Hazel' me, Darlene. You know that woman has had her hat set for Ed Hudson since the day she convinced him to give her a job at his insurance office, while poor little Sue Ann was sick and a dyin' from the cancer. Now, she's just flauntin' herself in front of him and actin' like she wants to be a mother to that little boy of his'n. And here, she's up and divorced Kenneth, a decent hard-workin' man. I've knowed his people my whole life. He's provided good for her and she's a leavin' him because she knows Ed's got something even better— she's a just tradin' up. Now, you've got her in here tonight with the little children, sewin' up the costumes for the Christmas play. That ripper don't have no place here in the house of the Lord, iffin' you ask me, and you orta know better. Why, you orta be ashamed of yoreself, Darlene."

"Hazel, let me tell you something. You don't know anything about what's going on with Sissy and Kenneth. You don't know how hard Sissy has tried to make her marriage work or what's been going on in her marriage. Rather than wagging your vicious tongue and spreading vile gossip, you might want to march yourself into the sanctuary and put yourself down in front of the altar. It sounds like to me you need some time on your knees to think about your sins!"

"Darlene Johnson, I don't have no sins. I ain't the one out chasing a man when his wife's not even been in the ground long enough for her body to git cold."

"There's more than one sin, Hazel. Seems to me I remember a verse in the Bible that says, 'Judge not lest ye be judged.' Ever thought about that one, Hazel?"

"Well," Mrs. Griffin snorts, "I guess you've just let that Sissy Maiden convince you adultery is fine and dandy, Darlene. Yore mama and daddy shore will be proud to hear of that."

"You know what, Hazel? My mama and daddy are just fine with me not sticking my nose where it doesn't belong. You ought to try it some time!"

Oh, my goodness! Who would have thought? Momma is more like Grandma than she thinks. Why, she just told off Hazel Griffin right here in the church. I sure can't wait to see Grandma's face when she hears about this. I hope it's not gossiping if I happen to be the one to tell her. But, even if it is, I still can't wait to see the look on her face. Oops. Sorry, Jesus.

Oh, shoot. Mrs. Griffin charges right past me without looking. Whew, that was close. I guess I'd better head out to get my coat before Momma catches me. She probably wouldn't be too happy to find me listening in on her and Mrs. Griffin.

"Darlene."

Wait a minute, that sounds like Mrs. Maiden.

"Oh, Sissy, oh my, I'm so sorry. Please don't cry. Come here."

"Darlene," Mrs. Maiden lets out a pitiful sob. Oh, no. This is just awful. I bet she heard every word that hateful old Mrs. Griffin said. I just hate that old biddy. Oops, sorry again, Jesus, but Mrs. Griffin was being mean about Mrs. Maiden. I like Mrs. Maiden. She's a real nice person and pretty, too.

"Darlene, I tried so hard. People just don't understand about Kenneth. You know I tried. I don't want everybody to know all my business, but if Hazel starts spreading these kinds of rumors, am I going to have to tell the truth about Kenneth? What am I going to do?"

"Oh, Sissy, you're not going to do anything for the time being. Look, Hazel Griffin is just one spiteful old woman with nothing better to talk about. She'll get tired of you eventually and leave you alone. She's a schoolyard bully. If she finds out she can't get to you, she'll move on. I promise."

"I sure hope so. I should have come out here and defended myself. I just couldn't, Darlene."

"You don't have to defend yourself, Sissy. You haven't done anything wrong. You just remember that. Now, come on, dry your eyes and give me a hug."

Wow, that's just what Momma says to me and Timmy if we're crying. I think I must have the best momma in the whole wide world.

"Come on, Sissy, let's go get our coats and go on home. It's been a long, hard night and we have to be back here tomorrow night for the program."

Oh, shoot. I'd better scoot. I take off running down the hall before Momma and Mrs. Maiden have the chance to catch me. Whew, that was close. I know listening in is wrong, but sometimes I just can't seem to help myself. I hate to admit it, but I'm not sorry. I'd never find out anything if I didn't listen in sometimes. Funny thing is, though, I still don't know what Mrs. Maiden's husband did. It must have been something bad, because she is a good person. I just know it. I hope you do too, Jesus; seems like to me Mrs. Maiden just might need a friend right now. I hope she's okay. I sure did hate to hear her cry.

Tonight's my big night. I'm gonna be Mary in the Christmas play and Sammy Coleman's gonna be Joseph. Karen's had a heyday ribbing me about that one. But I don't care; well, maybe I do a little bit. Momma says it's an honor to play the mother of the sweet baby Jesus and shouldn't let anyone ruin it for me. But, I swear, if Karen even looks at me cross-eyed once tonight, she's gonna get it. Sorry, Jesus.

The best part about tonight is that my daddy is going to come to the church with us. I had a hard time believing it when Momma told me, but it makes me so happy. I know he won't be able to see me, but at least he'll be there. Momma said it might be easier for him to come to something like this, when everybody's attention will be on the program, and not him. I'm not sure what she means by that, but I know Daddy don't like to think people are looking at him, even though he can't see them. I guess it's just been hard on my daddy learning to be blind. Momma says this is a good sign, though. She thinks maybe Daddy is coming around and will get back to his old self real soon. At least that's what she said to me. She also told me that Daddy wanted to come tonight because he knew it meant a lot to me. He's right about that. I'm real glad he's coming.

"Emmybeth, it's time to go. We've got to get to the church so I can help everybody get into their costumes."

"Okay, Momma, I'm coming."

I get my costume from the hook on the back of my bedroom door and start toward the kitchen. Momma ironed my costume today, so I would look nice for the program. Timmy's in the kitchen trying to put on his coat when I walk in.

"Mary and Joseph sitting in a tree . . ."

"Timmy, you little jerk!" I scream just as Daddy walks into the room behind me, tapping his white cane.

"Emmybeth, Timmy, now come on, let's not have no fussin' here on Christmas Eve. You might do well to remember Santa Claus has done left the North Pole and is on his way. He just might change his mind and skip over this house if he hears fussin' and fightin' goin' on."

"He started it, Daddy," I proclaim.

"She's the one that likes Sammy, Daddy, you know she does."

"Enough."

"What's going on in here?"

"Nothing, Darlene," Daddy chuckles, "Just a little skirmish. Business as usual. It's all taken care of. Right, Emmybeth? Right, Timmy?"

"Sure thing," I say without a lot of conviction.

"Daddy, can you ride me a pony?"

"Not right now, Timmy. Do you have your coat on? If you do, you can come on out to the car with me."

"Roger that, Daddy."

"I take that to mean yes. Come on, Timmy boy. Let's go."

Daddy and Timmy leave the kitchen and head out the door to the car. Wow. I can't believe it. Daddy seems almost like my old daddy. Maybe he is getting better.

"Momma."

"Yes, Emmy. Please tell me you have everything. We need to go. What is it?"

"I's just wondering."

"Oh, Emmybeth, come on now. I don't have time for a lot of talk. We need to go."

"Momma, I just wanted to know if you think Daddy's gonna be okay, tonight. I'm real happy he's going. I just want everything to be okay."

"Emmybeth, it'll be just fine. I promise. Your daddy didn't want to let you down. That's why he's coming. I think this is a positive step for your daddy. Now, come on, scoot. He's going to be just fine, and so are you."

We head out the door and get into the car with Daddy and Timmy. I sure hope it's all going to be okay. I wonder if

Daddy knows about Momma and Mrs. Griffin having a fuss last night. I know she didn't say anything to me about it. But then again, she wouldn't have. She hardly ever tells me the good stuff. She did go over to Grandma's early this morning. She let on that she was just going to help her with baking the applesauce cakes for tomorrow's Christmas dinner, but I just bet she went over there to talk to her about Hazel Griffin.

We're at the church before I know it. Timmy's been talking the whole way, but I've not been listening. He doesn't have a whole lot to say that I want to hear, anyway. Momma pulls the car around to the back of the church so we can go into the Sunday School classrooms where we're all going to get dressed for the play. I wonder what she'll do about Daddy. I'm not sure he can find his way to the sanctuary from here.

"Okay, kids, here we are. Emmybeth, make sure you've got everything you need for your costume. Timmy, I declare, you've got your coat off. It's not like it took us that long to get here. Put it back on, right now, and hang onto it when you get inside. It'll be colder when the program is over, and you'll need it. Vernon, wait right there. I'll come around and help you out."

"Darlene, I'm okay. Don't worry about me. Timmy will help me to the sanctuary. You and Emmybeth just go on and get ready for the program. You're gonna do good in your program, Emmybeth. Timmy and me will be toward the back of the church. You look for us, okay?"

"Okay, Daddy."

Daddy gets out of the car with his white cane. Timmy gets out of the backseat and takes Daddy's other hand as they begin a slow, awkward walk toward the back entrance of the church. I don't think it's Daddy's fault the walk is awkward. Timmy's the one that's wandering along.

"Momma," I say as I close the car door, "Do you think it's okay to let Daddy try to find the sanctuary on his own? I mean, what if he falls and gets hurt, or mad, or something?"

"Sweetie, he'll be just fine. We talked about this earlier and he told me he wanted to come here tonight. He just didn't want me to make a big deal about it or try to lead him around like he's an invalid. He's trying, Emmybeth. He's trying hard to do better. Most of all, he wanted to be here for you tonight. He knew this was important to you. He wanted to come."

"That's good, isn't it?"

"It's exceptionally good. Things are getting better. See, I promised you they would and slowly, but surely, they are. So, are you ready for your big debut?"

"I reckon, Momma. My stomach feels a little funny, though. "Do you reckon it's butterflies? You said that might happen."

"Probably, just take a deep breath and say a little prayer. You'll be all right. I promise."

"Gee, Momma, two promises," I smile at her, "You sure promise a lot."

"Well, Emmybeth, not only do I make promises, I keep them, too!"

I squeeze Momma's hand a little tighter as we enter the church doors and head to the classrooms. She really is the best. I hope I can make her proud tonight, and my daddy, too. Even if my daddy can't see me being Mary tonight, I'll talk real loud and make sure he hears me. It's the best thing

I can do for him, since he came here for me tonight. You know, he's as good of a daddy as momma is a mother. Now, if we could only work on making Timmy better. Oops. Sorry, Jesus. I'm not serious about that part—well, not real serious, anyway.

"Emmybeth, Emmybeth, come on, it's time to get up! Santa Claus came last night. He really, really did!! Yippee!"

Oh, my goodness! Timmy squealing and jumping on me is not exactly the best way to wake up on Christmas morning.

"Okay, Timmy, I'm coming. Just hold on a minute," I say as I climb out of bed and grab my robe from the bedpost.

"You'd better go get Momma and Daddy. You know they told us last night not to open our presents without them."

"Okay, okay. I'll go get 'em, but you hurry, Emmy!"

Timmy lets out another big squeal as he busts in Momma's and Daddy's bedroom. I'm betting they're happy about that. I run my brush through my hair quickly and wait with Timmy in the hallway, while Momma and Daddy get their robes.

"Okay, younguns, let's go and see what Santa brought last night."

We head down the hallway with Timmy leading the way. Momma and Daddy bring up the rear. Daddy seems like he's in a good mood this morning. I don't know what's going on with him, but at least he's smiling for a change.

"Oh, goody, goody gum drops," Timmy yells as he runs toward a shiny red bike. I guess Santa decided to bring him something after all.

"Momma, Daddy, lookey what Santa brought for me!"

"That's just great Timmy. Why don't you tell Daddy what your present from Santa looks like?"

"Okay, Momma. Sorry, Daddy, I forgot you can't see it. It's a red bicycle with strings hanging outta the handlebars and some extra wheels on the back so's I won't fall over when I ride."

"That's sounds like just what you needed, Timmy boy. What about a horn? Do you see a horn on that good lookin' ride?"

"Let's see, Daddy. Oh, yeah!" Timmy lets out another big squeal and honks the horn three times in a row.

"Okay, Timmy, okay," Daddy laughs, "Emmybeth, honey, you tell Daddy what Santa left for you."

"Let's see, Daddy," I go sit down beside my gifts, so I can begin to describe them to Daddy. I'm just not sure how to begin.

"Emmybeth," Momma chimes in, "I think Santa must think you've been a real good girl this year. I don't think I've ever seen such a pretty coat, and just look at those boots."

I guess Momma can see this is a little bit hard for me. I never dreamed Santa would really bring me the midi-length, brown furry coat I picked out of the Sears catalog, much less the white, knee-high boots I've been wanting since it got wintertime. I was afraid to even hope for it since Daddy's not working, and Momma's just got started at the store.

"Daddy, Santa Claus brought me the coat I've been wanting, and some boots, too. The coat is so soft. It's fur, well, not real fur, but, you know what I mean? I guess, uh, Daddy, uh, you want me to bring it over there so you can feel it?" Man, I hope he don't get mad at me for asking.

"Emmybeth, I think that's a real good idea. I might not be able to see you in your purty little coat, but I can know how good it feels. Bring it here."

I walk over to Daddy and he reaches out his hand. I take his hand and rub it over my new coat. Daddy touches the coat, then reaches out both arms toward me and pulls me into a hug.

"Emmybeth," he whispers in my ear, "I'm so glad Santa knew exactly what to get you. You've been a real good girl this year. A real trooper. I love you, sweetpea."

"I love you, too, Daddy," I say as the tears come into my eyes.

"Okay, now, kids, it's Momma's turn," Daddy releases me from his hug, and I look up into my Momma's smiling face.

"My turn, oh, Vernon, what do you mean? Santa doesn't bring presents for the grownups."

"No, that's right, but your husband just might have something for you. I believe it's kindly behind the tree, hidden back a little ways. That's if my helper put it where I told him to."

"Your helper, what do you mean?"

"Well, just wait a minute. You go ahead and open your present; then I'll tell you how it got here. It's a right funny story."

Momma goes around to the back of the tree, and sure enough there's a gift for her from Daddy. She comes back around and sits on the couch with Daddy to open it. Timmy and me watch her as she undoes the paper.

"What'cha got, Momma?" Timmy asks.

"I don't know, Timmy, let's see."

Momma finishes unwrapping her gift and lets out a little yip.

"Oh, Vernon, you remembered! You used to buy this perfume for me when we were first married. Emmybeth, Timmy it's called White Shoulders. I haven't had any of this in years. Vernon, what made you remember, and how on earth did you get this? I don't remember us being anywhere you could have gotten it."

"Well, now, that's a right funny story. Now, you see, I was thinkin' what I could get ya' that would be special, after all you've had to take on this year. Then, I remembered how you used to like this particular perfume so much. So, I decided since it'd been awhile since you'd had any, you might enjoy having some again. Problem was, I certainly didn't want to ask you to go get it. So, one day last week when Junior stopped by and y'all was down at the store, I decided to ask him to go get it. He agreed to do it, because he wanted to help me, but, then he got afraid somebody would see him buying perfume and get the wrong idea and think he had a sweetheart," Daddy chuckles. "But, he went anyways. He swore the girl at the counter looked at him funny when he asked for women's perfume. I declare, that boy's just plumb silly sometimes. But, he did me the favor. He even got the perfume wrapped up for me at the store, and I was mighty obliged. I sure do hope you enjoy wearing it, but don't let onto Junior that I told y'all he's the one who went and got it."

"Daddy, you haven't opened your gift from Momma, and Emmybeth and me. You want me to get it?"

Leave it to Timmy to butt in like that—I think it was sweet of my daddy to get my momma her favorite perfume. Why, it's almost romantic, like something you'd see on television.

"Sure thing, Timmy, bring it here."

Timmy goes and gets our gift to Daddy. I wonder how he's gonna do this?

"Okay, Timmy, let's see, hand it here, now," Daddy takes the package from Timmy.

"I tell you what, Timmy, I'll open it, and then you tell me what it is. We'll do it together, all right?"

"All right, Daddy," Timmy's getting excited and hopping around, although I'm not sure the gift is all that exciting.

Daddy takes the paper off just as Timmy blurts out what it is to him; well, actually to the whole county as loud as Timmy yells.

"It's a record album, Daddy, a new one for your record player!"

"Well, all right, Timmy, that's mighty nice. You know, I's gettin' tired of listening to the same ones, so, I really needed this. Thank you, Timmy, and you too, Emmybeth, and Darlene. Thank you to everybody. Now, Timmy, let Emmybeth read to me just who's on this record."

"Okay, Daddy, read it Emmybeth, read it!"

I guess I am the best choice for this job, especially since wild boy can't read.

"Daddy, it's a Johnny Cash record. We knew you liked him best."

"That's right, I do. Well, y'all did well. I'm lookin' forward to listenin' to this. No wonder ole' Santa Claus noticed what good youngun's live at this house. I guess that's why he left exactly what you two wanted. Don't you think so, Darlene?"

"I sure do. Now, I think I'll go out to the kitchen, and make some pancakes. Emmybeth, you want to help me?"

"Sure, Momma, I'll help."

With that, we leave the room while Timmy starts telling Daddy more about his new bike. I hope the rest of this day goes as good as this. Although, I'm not sure it could get much better than having my daddy act like he used to. That's the best Christmas gift of all. Thank you, Santa Claus, and thank you, too, Jesus.

After we fill up on pancakes, Momma starts fixing the food she's gonna take over to Grandma's and Grandpop's for lunch. She told me to come in here to the bathroom to get Timmy washed up and ready to go. So, it's my job to get nasty boy's face clean, and help him into his clothes. We always have to wear church clothes on holidays. I like to because I'm more grownup. Timmy's just a little pain about it. Sorry, Jesus, but he is.

"Timmy, I'm not going to tell you one more time. Momma said for you to get your good clothes on, and that means putting on this tie. Now, don't make me tell you one more time, young man."

"Don't you tell me what to do Smarty Pants. You're not the boss of me."

"I am too. Momma said so. Now, don't you make me go get her, because you'll be in big trouble, then. Momma and Daddy might even send your bicycle back to Santa Claus at the North Pole."

Take that, you little freak. It doesn't really scare him, though. He just sticks his tongue out at me while I clip on his tie. But since I don't want nothing to ruin this day, I just ignore him and keep on dressing him.

"Now, go on; and don't get dirty before we leave. Momma's trying to get the food ready, so you behave, Timmy!"

He's still sticking out his tongue at me as he leaves the bathroom and goes back to the den. Who cares? This morning was just so great. I'm not gonna let him ruin it. I close the bathroom door so I can have some privacy and lock it, too. I'm not going to take a chance on Timmy running back in here and bothering me. I open the cabinet door underneath the sink and take out a washcloth. I wash my face and brush my teeth. I look in the mirror and wish one more time that my hair could be golden blond, like Jan Brady's, but I guess that's not gonna happen. Today I don't care quite so much though. I guess some things are better than having golden blond hair. Having a daddy that's happy again is one of them.

When I finish in the bathroom I go back to my room and put on my red and blue plaid dress. It looks kind of like Christmas, and it's not a hand-me-down from my pain-in-the butt cousin, Katherine. At least she won't be at Grandma's and Grandpop's today. They go to her other grandparents' house down in Knoxville for Christmas, so they send their gifts early so we can open them on Christmas day. I don't especially like Katherine, or my Aunt Flora and Uncle Earl, but they do send good gifts. I hope that's okay. I mean, I guess it could be considered unchristian, to like their gifts, but be glad they're not coming. Maybe I'll ask Grandma about that sometime.

"Emmybeth, come on. As soon as I get my dress on, we're going be ready to leave," Momma yells from her bedroom.

"All right, Momma, I'm gonna put on my new boots and coat. Is that all right?"

"Of course, Emmybeth, they're yours to wear wherever you want."

I go to the den to put on my new boots and coat. Timmy and Daddy are in the kitchen getting on their coats. I can't wait to show Grandma what I look like in my new clothes. Momma walks into the den as I finish buttoning up coat.

"What do you think, Momma? Does this look okay?"

"It sure does, Emmybeth. You look like a teenager in your fancy boots and fur coat."

"Oh, Momma, you know I'm not a teenager."

"Yes, but you are growing up, Emmy; growing up to be quite the young lady."

I can feel my cheeks get hot from hearing Momma's compliment.

"Ready to go?"

"Yes, m'am. Are we gonna walk over to Grandma's?" I'm not too crazy about the idea of getting mud on my new boots first trip out of the house in them.

"No, sweetie, I've got too much food to carry for that. We'll just load the car and drive over."

"Okay."

Momma gives me a quick hug and we walk toward the kitchen. I'm just so excited. This is shaping up to be one of the best Christmas days ever!

Chapter 13

Man, I can't wait for springtime. It's freezing cold, so I run across the parking lot as fast as I can to the store. Junior's not even smoking a cigarette outside this afternoon like he usually is, right about the time I get off the school bus every afternoon. But, I guess it's too cold for him this afternoon. Momma says it's just a little more than three weeks 'til springtime. Even though the crocuses are coming up in our front yard, it still feels an awful lot like winter to me. I hope Momma's right, and it warms up, soon.

Jing-a-ling. I cannot believe my eyes. Papaw Jack is sitting behind the counter with Miss Hawkins. They had their heads hunched together super close, but they jerked them up real fast when the bell jingled as I came through the door.

"Papaw Jack, what are you doing here? Uh, hello, Miss Hawkins; uh, Papaw Jack is Momma okay?"

"Oh, she's fine. Now, don't ya' go to worryin' youngun.' She's jest gone to Johnson City to take yore daddy for his doctor's appointment. Didn't she tell ya' this mornin'?"

"That's right, Papaw Jack. She told me. I reckon I just forgot."

"How are you doing, Miss Emmybeth? I swear, Jack, isn't your granddaughter just turning into the prettiest little thing?" Miss Hawkins turns to my papaw, and I swear if she don't giggle! There's something really wrong with her lately.

"She shore is. Why, one day she might be as purty as another young lady I know."

"Oh, now, hush up!"

Oh, my goodness. I think I'm gonna puke. What am I gonna do if I have to stand here and listen to this all afternoon?

"Well, uh, Papaw Jack, I think I'm gonna go to the back and have some coffee. Momma lets me do that of the afternoon."

"Okay, Emmybeth. I'm just gonna sit next to this here heater and try to stay warm. Myrtle, I mean, Miss Hawkins, brought this here heater back for me after she finished up her shift earlier today. She didn't want the cold to make my ole' crippled legs hurt. Now, we've got a heater in the back, and one here up in the front, so we can all stay warm. That right, Myrtle?"

"Oh, now, Jack, you know it wasn't no trouble at all. I just want you to be comfortable."

I head on toward the back of the store before I start gagging over the way those two are talking to each other. Papaw Jack didn't even remember to give me a Starlite mint like he usually does. He was too busy paying attention to Miss Hawkins. You don't reckon they're boyfriend and girlfriend? Why, that would be disgusting. They're like really old. Why, Papaw Jack's in his fifties. Wonder what Grandma would have to say about this? I'm not sure I could even tell her without throwing up all over myself. Yuck! Double yuck!!

I go to the coffee pot and start to pour myself a cup of coffee when the bell rings again at the front of the store. I turn around to see who it is. Why, it's that hateful old Hazel Griffin from church. I never have forgiven her for what I heard her say to Momma about Mrs. Maiden the night before the Christmas program. I sure hope she doesn't come back here. I don't even want to have to say hello to her. Although Momma told me I should speak to all the customers, even the ones I don't like. She says that's just part of being in business. I reckon it is, but it don't mean I have to like it.

"Afternoon, Jack, Myrtle. Where's Darlene? She off flittin' around Johnson City with that little hussy Sissy Maiden? Why, Jack, I know yore boy's done gone blind, but he orta know that the God-fearin' people here in Ivy Creek don't think much of Darlene upholdin' that ripper. Why, she got plumb huffy with me in church afore Christmas, defendin' that Sissy. I'm here to tell you, I didn't like her tone not one bit, I tell you what, not one little bit."

"Now, Hazel . . ."

"Jack, let me handle this." Miss Hawkins butts in. No surprise, there.

"Hazel, let me tell you something. You can just take your gossipy old self somewhere else and tell your story to somebody that wants to hear it. You don't know nothin' about nothin.' Of course, some things never change. You never have knowed nothing about anything. You just think you know. Sissy Maiden is a fine girl. Sissy and Darlene and all the girls in the sewing circle have come to mean a lot to me this past year. Everybody in Ivy Creek knows the score on Kenneth Maiden. Of course, it was everybody in Ivy Creek, except poor little Sissy, until she wised up and saw the truth about him. He's been out cattin' around since Day One. Just because he grew up in Ivy Creek, and Sissy didn't, you think you've got to defend him, and not her. I'm here to tell you, I am sick and tired of hearing everybody repeat what you've been saying about Sissy. You can just shut your big fat lying trap. How do you like them apples, old girl?"

"Well, I never," sputters Mrs. Griffin.

"And you ain't goin' to neither. Now, go on, get. And don't come back 'til you've learned to keep your mouth shut!"

Mrs. Griffin turns around and goes out the door. She slams it so hard that the bell keeps ringing a lot longer than it usually does.

"Myrtle Hawkins, you shore are a feisty thing, once you git started," Papaw Jack says as he laughs real hard and slaps his knee. "Did you see the look on that old heifer's face? Why, I'd give my pickup truck to have a pitcher of that!"

"Well, Jack, sometimes a girl's just gotta do, what a girl's gotta do!"

"You know, Myrtle, I jest think you might be the best old girl in Ivy Creek! Yessiree! I do."

Oh, my goodness! I cannot believe my ears . . . or my eyes. Papaw Jack just laid a big kiss right on Miss Hawkins. It's a good thing I haven't taken a drink of my coffee yet, or I'd have to spit it out right here and now! At best, I think my eyes may burn up right in my head. Oh, Lord. Sorry, Jesus. But did you see that, too?

"Hold on there, feller. I believe there's a little miss looking on from the back of the store."

Oh, shoot. I was hoping they wouldn't remember I was here. Oh, no. They're gonna know I saw them kissing. Oh, Lord. Shoot. Sorry again, Jesus.

Jing-a-ling. Here comes my momma into the store just in time. Thank you, Jesus, and I really do mean that. Maybe she'll get me out of here before I have to admit I saw them kissing.

"Jack, Miss Hawkins, was that Hazel Griffin I saw tearing out of the parking lot just now? She was driving like a maniac. What's going on with her today?"

"Oh, nothing that Myrtle couldn't handle," Papaw Jack says as he starts laughing again.

"Darlene, you know better than anybody what she's been going around saying all over Ivy Creek. Now, I'm sorry, I may have run off one of your customers, but I just had to tell Hazel, in no uncertain terms, she needs to quit spreadin' rumors. I thought I handled it well. Jack's just exaggerating. You know how men are."

She turns and giggles at Papaw Jack again. I swear I will puke if they kiss for a second time.

"You know, Miss Hawkins, if she quits telling tales, it'll be worth it. I'll gladly give up her business. By the way, what are you still doing here? I thought you were going on home once Jack got here."

"Well, Darlene, uh, uh," Miss Hawkins stutters like she don't know what to say. Bet that's a first.

"Darlene, Myrtle was nice enough to go fetch us a second heater from her place and bring it back down here to the store. Ya' see, it's mighty cold in here today, and we needed the one heater in the back to keep it warm there. But then, ya' see, my legs woulda got to achin', and well, Myrtle said she jest couldn't stand the thoughts of that," Papaw Jack's voice trails off.

"Oh, I see," says Momma, but I know she hasn't seen near what I've seen this afternoon. My eyes still feel like they're burning from seeing that kiss.

"Well, I'm glad you did that, Miss Hawkins. Jack, if you can stay just a few more minutes, I'm gonna run Vernon and Emmybeth to the house. I'll come back and close up."

"No, no, now, Darlene, you jest run on home. We'll, I mean, I'll be happy to close up."

"Are you sure, Jack? I know you don't like to be out in this cold weather."

I swear I can see a hint of a grin on Momma's face when she looks at Papaw Jack and Miss Hawkins.

"No, now that we've got both these heaters runnin', it's just fine and dandy in here. My legs are A-Okay. You need to go on home and git supper for Vernon and them younguns. I know they're hungry, and yore probably tired after sittin' in the doctor's office this afternoon. Did the doctor say everything's okay with Vernon?"

"Yes, he's doing fine. I guess you're right, Jack. I would like to go home and get settled in for the evening. It would be a nice change; seems like I do get tired more easily these days. Well, come on, Emmybeth, let's head to the house. Don't forget your schoolbooks. Have a good evening, Jack; you, too, Miss Hawkins."

"Evening, Darlene, Emmybeth. You make sure you tell Vernon, and that precious little boy of yours I said, 'hello.'"

Oh, brother. I'm not even believing she just called Timmy "precious." Man, just last summer she told Momma all about how Timmy was yanking on Grandpop at the church picnic. She said Timmy was wanting Grandpop to take him to the dessert table, and that Timmy might just get tubby if she didn't watch out. She sure didn't think he was "precious" then. Maybe she just wants Papaw Jack to keep liking her.

We walk across the parking lot. Momma opens the door and gets into the driver's seat, while I climb into the back seat right behind her.

"Hello, Daddy."

"Hey there; how's my big girl this afternoon?"

"I'm fine."

"Did you have a good day at school?"

"Yes, sir."

"Vernon, your daddy said he'd close up. He said just go on home and get dinner for you and the children. Miss Hawkins was there with him. I guess she's going to help him close. You think?"

"I guess," Daddy says smiling.

"Don't you think that's interesting?"

"Oh, Darlene, don't be makin' too much of it."

"Papaw Jack kissed Miss Hawkins right on the mouth and I saw it!"

Oh, no. I can't believe I just said that out loud to my momma and daddy.

"What?!" Momma exclaims.

"Emmybeth, are you sure you saw that? Now, don't be saying things you're not sure about."

"I swear it's the truth, Daddy. I double-dog swear it!"

"Emmybeth, don't swear! I don't know what to say about what you witnessed between Papaw Jack and Miss Hawkins, but don't you 'double-dog swear' anything. It's not ladylike."

"Momma, I want you to know I'm telling the truth is all. I know you think swearing on it is unladylike, but Daddy wasn't believing me otherwise."

"Just calm down, Darlene. Now, Emmybeth, tell Daddy again what you saw, or what you think you saw. I know you'll tell me the truth. Daddy and Momma know you're a good girl."

"I'm telling you, I saw Papaw Jack kiss Miss Hawkins. It was right after she told off Hazel Griffin for talking bad about Sissy Maiden and Momma."

"Me, what'd she say about me? What have I done?"

"Mrs. Griffin don't like it that you defended Mrs. Maiden to her, that's all. So, Myrtle, I mean, Miss Hawkins just told her what for. It almost made me like Miss Hawkins 'til I saw Papaw Jack kiss her. Then I just wanted to puke!"

"Emily Beth Johnson, I declare! Watch your tongue young lady!"

Momma is trying to act like she means it, but Daddy's laughing now, and she starts laughing too.

"Momma, it really did make me kinda sick."

"I know, sweetie. I'm sure it did," Momma says, and just keeps on laughing.

I'm glad they think this is so funny. I sure don't. I'm not sure if I'll ever see what's funny about Papaw Jack kissing on

Miss Hawkins. I bet you Grandma won't laugh either. Maybe she'll have some sense about this because even though I love my momma and daddy more than anybody, and I don't want to be disrespectful—they're just acting plumb crazy about a nasty old kiss. Yuck! And I'm not sorry about thinking that, Jesus!

When we get to the house Momma and Daddy are still laughing. I still don't see what they think is so funny about Papaw Jack and Miss Hawkins.

"Emmybeth, run over to Grandma's and get Timmy for me, all right? And don't be dragging your feet getting back home. Supper'll be ready in just a few minutes. We're going to have hamburgers and French fries tonight. I can have that ready in no time. I took the hamburger out of the freezer and put it in the refrigerator to thaw this morning before I went to the store. Run along. I'll carry your books inside for you."

I start across the field to Grandma's when Momma yells for me to come back. I run back to where she's standing just outside the kitchen door.

"Do you need me to bring something back from Grandma's?"

"No, Emmybeth. I just wanted to tell you to keep what you saw at the store to yourself. Understand me?"

"Oh, all right, Momma," I say and turn around to head back toward Grandma's.

Shoot. Sorry, Jesus. I sure did want to tell Grandma about Papaw Jack and Miss Hawkins. Leave it to Momma to read my mind. I know better than to argue with her. And I don't want to get in trouble.

Well, I guess it's for the best. Grandma might have had a heart attack when I told her, and I sure don't want nothing happening to my Grandma. I bet Momma'll tell her when I'm not around. I sure would like to hear what my Grandma has to say about Papaw Jack and Miss Hawkins kissing. I bet she won't laugh like Momma and Daddy did when I told them. I bet she'll have plenty to say.

I just hate the thoughts of missing out on it. I'm always missing out on the good stuff. Well, shoot! Sorry, Jesus. Guess I'd better go get Timmy, and keep my mouth shut.

Chapter 14

Today is the day I've been waiting for. Momma is going to finish my Easter dress tonight after supper. All that's left to do is put the lace around the collar, and she promised me she would show me how to embroider two pink flowers on each of the dress pockets after she finishes the lace. I hope she feels like doing it tonight. We were supposed to do it last night, but she was just too tired when she got home from the store and got supper cooked.

Most nights, I've been doing the dishes after we eat, just because I can tell Momma's really worn out. Timmy even tries to help; but he usually causes more work for me in the end. I try to be nice about it, though. I know when I get to fussing with Timmy it gets on Momma's nerves. I can tell. Daddy does come out to the table to eat most every night now, but he always goes back to the den as soon as he eats. It's not like he can help me with the dishes anyway.

I rode the bus home this afternoon, instead of going to the store. I figured if I went ahead and got all of my homework finished, and got the table set, then all's Momma will have to do is cook supper when she gets in. After we finish supper, then we can work on my dress. I might even try to bring up my birthday to her tonight; after all it's coming up next month and I've got some ideas about my present.

I hollered at Daddy when I got home, to let him know I was here; but he didn't answer. I just got me some vanilla wafers, and a glass of milk, and come on in here to my bedroom to finish my homework.

It's gotten a whole lot easier to be around Daddy these past couple of months; more than it used to be when he first got blind. I don't get near as uncomfortable as I used to when I would try to talk to him. He's still doesn't work around the house like he used to before the accident, but maybe he will someday. At least, maybe he'll work on things he can do, even though he's blind. I'm just not sure what that would be.

Creak. The back door swings open. I wonder who that is?

"Vernon, Vernon Johnson. You git on out here, son. We need to talk, right now."

Oh, my goodness! That's Papaw Jack. He sounds like he's angry. Oh, I hope him and Daddy don't fuss like they did the day Daddy come home from the hospital. It scared me so bad. Maybe I'll just stay in here 'til I know what's going on.

"Vernon, I mean it. Git on out here! It's time we had us a talk."

I can hear Daddy's cane tapping down the hallway.

"What's the matter, old man? I was sleeping. You don't have to holler so loud."

Daddy don't sound too happy either. Of course, that could be because he just woke up.

"Vernon, I've been a' stewin' on this all day. Well, I reckon I've been stewin' on this longer than that. I know ya' can't see no more, and that's got to be plumb awful, but you're gonna have to git yore head in the game and notice what's goin' on right before ya'. I's up to the store this mornin', and I'm here to tell ya', poor little Darlene looks like death warmed over. She's run down and tired, and yore just layin' up here on yore ass, lettin' her do all the work of the store, and keepin' tabs on Junior, too. I told ya' from the beginning, I can't be down there every day. I'm an old man, past my prime; but you're still able to git up and git out. I knowed a' lost your sight in that accident, but I'm here to tell ya', Vernon, I'm ashamed of ya'. I didn't know ya' lost yore spine too!"

"Well, old man, I reckon you've had a lot on your mind to come here to my house and say all that."

"Yeah, I reckon I have."

"You know what, old man . . . you are exactly right. I've not been pullin' my weight around here, and that's getting' ready to change."

"Now, hold on, what do you mean, Vernon? You're agreein' with me? I thought you'd be mad at me for sayin' my mind, shore as shootin'!"

"Aw, Daddy, you're right. I've knowed all along I's gonna have to git back at it, sooner or later. I just didn't know how to go about it. Them doctors over at the hospital have been tryin' to git me to go a place that helps people like me who've lost their eyesight. They'll school me in how to get along since I can't see, now. I've just fought them on it, until now. Listen, we was gonna tell Claude and Esther tonight when they come over to eat supper with us. I's supposed to call you earlier, and let you know to come, too. I tried you on the phone two or three times, but the line was busy and I couldn't git through to you. We've got some other news, too. It's the reason why I know I need to git back to work. Well, Darlene'll kill me if I tell you the rest. Just come on back here for supper, and we'll tell everybody at the same time."

"Well, uh, Vernon, would ya' reckon Darlene would care iffin' I brung one more mouth to feed? Well, uh, I might jest have somethin' I need to tell y'all, too."

"Keepin' secrets of your own, old man?" Daddy laughs.

"No, no, jest somethin' I need to tell y'all. The younguns too."

"Well, then, just bring your somebody with you then. We'll eat at the usual time."

"Ya' know, son, I'm right proud of ya'. I knew I raised ya' to have some spirit about ya'. I know it's hard on a man, too, when his body gits hurt. It crushed my heart as well as my legs when I had my accident. I don't know why the Good Lord saw fit to do the same thing to you, I mean, with yore accident. But we jest do the best we can, son. You'll git it all on the right track sooner or later. I got faith in ya', Vernon."

"Aw, old man, don't go gittin' all sentimental on me. It don't suit you." Daddy laughs again.

"I'll be back after while."

"See you, then. Git it, see ya'!"

Papaw Jack laughs, and the door slams shut.

"Emmybeth, you can come out, now."

I walk down the hallway to the kitchen. How'd he know I was here? I thought he said he was asleep when Papaw Jack came in.

"Yes, Daddy, did you need me to get you a Coca-Cola?"

"No, Emmybeth, I don't need anything to drink. If I did, I'd get it myself. I just wanted you to know that I knew you was here."

"Oh, well, um."

"It's okay," Daddy shakes his finger toward me, "Emmybeth, if you keep listenin' in on other people's conversations, sooner or later you're gonna hear something you don't want to!"

"Oh, Daddy, I doubt that'll ever happen!"

"Emily Beth. Oh, just come here and give me a hug!" Daddy laughs, and so do I. I don't know what the rest of the news will be at supper tonight, but if my daddy is happy, then so am I. Whatever it is, it must be good. Of course, I don't know what could be better than Daddy going back to work, and Momma not being tired all the time. For once, I may just have to wait and see.

"Daddy, would you say grace for us?"

"You know, Darlene, if Claude wouldn't mind, I think I might just like to say grace this evening."

"Vernon, you go right ahead, it's your house and a man's got a right to say grace at his own table."

"Thank you, Claude. Let's all bow our heads."

Everybody bows their head, including me this time. I don't want to have to look at Miss Hawkins looking all mooney-eyed at Papaw Jack anymore. I couldn't believe it when she came in with Papaw Jack tonight. I tried to warn Grandma, but she just shushed me when I tried to whisper in her ear. There's something funny about all this if you ask me. As usual, no one does.

"Dear Heavenly Father, we are truly grateful to you as we gather at your bountiful table this evening. We praise you for our many blessings. And dear Lord, while we may not understand all of the trials life hands us, we thank you for your grace and guidance as we make our way through. We ask your continued blessings on this family. In the name of your Son, Jesus Christ, we pray. Amen."

"Well, now, Vernon, I reckon that's better than I could have done," Grandpop says.

"Darlene, start passing the food around and I'll just go ahead and tell everybody the first part of our news, if you don't mind."

"You go ahead, Vernon. Mama, don't get up, you need to hear this too. We'll get Emmybeth's and Timmy's milk poured here in a minute."

"All right. What are y'all so fired up about that you've got us over here for supper in the middle of the week?"

Daddy clears his throat and starts talking.

"Y'all know this past year's been awful hard on me, and especially hard on Darlene and the younguns. Part of that I could have done better with, and part of it couldn't be helped. But, I know I've got to git back to work and help out so Darlene doesn't have to do everything by herself. I've decided to go to this school up in the northern part of the state. They've got people there who can teach me how to do all I need to git by in the world, even though I ain't never gonna be able to see again. I'll be there for about six weeks, so we'll have to rely on all y'all to help us out just a little bit longer. But when I git back, I should be able to run the store by myself for the most part. Of course, I'll have Junior there with me, runnin' the garage. Darlene says she still wants to be there part of the time running things too, just not all of the time like she is now. Darlene's turned out to be quite a good businesswoman, and she's sure got the store off and running to a good start. Turns out we shoulda been selling groceries all along."

"Well, now, that's some good news, Vernon. Claude and me's real proud of what Darlene's done with the grocery store. But, you're right. She's takin' on too much. She needs to get more rest. Darlene, you've looked peaked here, lately. I guess you're just worn out."

"Thanks, Mama, that's just what a woman always wants to hear. You know, how bad she's looking."

"Now, Darlene, I think Esther's right to be concerned about you. That's a mother's prerogative."

Good grief. If Miss Hawkins has started agreeing with my grandma, it won't be long 'til the end of time gets here.

"Y'all, there's a reason I'm looking so tired these days. It should get here sometime in August."

"Oh, Darlene, I do declare," Miss Hawkins says, "Does that mean what I think it does?"

"It sure does, Miss Hawkins. Mama, Daddy, Jack, how do you feel about adding another grandchild to the family?"

"Oh, my goodness. Well, Darlene, things must be going better between you and Vernon!"

"Mama, really, the children are sitting right here!"

I don't know what she means by that, but if my grandparents are getting another grandchild, I must be getting another brother or sister!

"Momma, momma, what's your news?"

Oh, of course Timmy doesn't get it; he hardly ever does.

"Well, Timmy, by the end of the summer, you're going to have a new baby brother or sister. Won't that be fun?"

"Well, just so long as I don't have to change its diapers. I guess, so. May I have some mashed potatoes?"

"Sure thing, Timmy, just pass your plate."

Momma smiles as Timmy passes his plate to her, then turns to me.

"What about you, Emmybeth? Ready for another brother, or sister?"

"I think I want a baby sister this time, Momma."

"Yeah, Darlene, see what you can do about that." Daddy laughs.

"Oh, this is just so exciting!" says Miss Hawkins as she grabs hold of Papaw Jack's hand—right here at the dinner table! I swear she's really starting to get on my nerves. She's not even family. I don't even know why she's here tonight.

"Well, Darlene, Vernon, not to try to steal the spotlight from y'all and yore good news, but, I've, I mean, we've got some news of our own."

Oh, no. What news could Papaw Jack and Miss Hawkins possibly have to tell us? You don't reckon they're gonna tell everybody that they're boyfriend and girlfriend? I really will just throw myself into the bowl of mashed potatoes if that's what they do. I mean, really, now, do they have to go ruining everybody's meal? If they kiss, I'll puke.

"Well, I never did plan on doing this again in my lifetime. But y'all know it's been a lot a years since May passed on, and well, shoot, you tell 'em, Myrtle."

"Jack and me's gonna get married, and he's moving up to my house to help me take care of the farm!"

Eeewww! I am gonna puke! Miss Hawkins is gonna be my grandma. I'd rather kiss Sammy Coleman in front of the whole fourth grade!

"Well, old man, come here and shake my hand. Miss Hawkins, welcome to the family!"

My daddy is welcoming Miss Hawkins to the family. What next?

"Myrtle, old girl, didn't know you had it in you! Come here and give me a hug!"

Grandma, too! I think I'm gonna die. I'm just gonna die.

"Emmybeth," Momma says placing her hand on my shoulder, "Why don't you and Timmy go give Miss Hawkins a hug? She's going to be part of our family, now."

"Oh, Darlene, honey, don't be calling me Miss Hawkins, no more, I'm just plain ole' Myrtle. And that goes for Emmybeth and Timmy, too, lessen' y'all younguns want to call me Granny Myrtle. I think I'd like that just fine!"

I get up and go around the table to hug Miss Hawkins, I mean, Granny Myrtle. Reckon I could ever call her that, and not want to throw myself out the nearest window?

"Granny Myrtle, Granny Myrtle," Timmy yells, and hugs her so hard I'm pretty sure it knocks the wind out of her just a little bit.

"Oh, you sweet little boy. I never thought I'd have any grandyounguns. Now, I'm going to have three living right down the road from me! Come here, Emmybeth, and give your new granny a hug."

"Yes, Emmybeth, hug your new granny. I don't mind sharing, really, I don't," Grandma says as I walk past her chair to get to Miss Hawkins. I hug Miss Hawkins, I mean, Granny Myrtle, and make my way back to my chair.

"Well, I reckon if there's no more news, we'd better eat before our food gets cold," Daddy says, as we all sit down again around the table.

Grownups! Now, I know I'll never figure them out.

I can't remember when there's ever been so much laughing and hugging in our house as there was tonight. I know I'm happy about the new baby. It's fun when I go over to Karen's, and her mama lets us watch John Michael. Of course, he doesn't do much except smile and giggle when we make funny faces at him, but he's okay. I hope our new baby will be like that.

As for Papaw Jack marrying again, well, he seems happy. So does my daddy. I guess I'll get use to Miss Hawkins being my Granny Myrtle. I guess I don't have any choice. Okay, Jesus. I'm trying to be good about this. I sure hope you'll be there to help me through it.

Chapter 15

I am just so excited. The ladies from the church are finally meeting at our house again, and today it's time for me to rejoin The Ivy Creek Sewing Circle; even though they won't know it, I sure will. I took Timmy down to Grandma's and Grandpop's early, and I'm already back and ready to get into my hiding place. Grandma said since I was so fidgety, I could run back up here, and she'd come in a few minutes. Momma's still in the bathroom.

I think she's throwing up again. She does that most every morning now; but Grandma says not to worry. She says morning sickness don't last forever. It's just plumb gross if you ask me; but, as usual, no one does.

Let's see. I'll just open up the door and push back these cans of beans. Now, wait a minute, I can shove everything here to the side, and scoot right in. Ouch! Durn it! Sorry, Jesus. Oh, man. It's so crowded in here. Shoot, there goes a can rolling across the kitchen floor. Now, I'll have to get out and go catch it so the ladies won't find a stray can of beans on the floor when they get here.

I try scooting out of the cabinet back onto the kitchen floor. Shoot! Sorry, Jesus. I hit my stupid head again. What's the problem here? I never had trouble getting in here before. Wait a minute, I think, as I sit in front of the cabinet rubbing my head.

You know, when they measured us in gym the last week of school, I had grown a whole two inches since the first of school. I also weigh five pounds more than I did last September when I went for my physical with Dr. Morgan. Oh, no. You don't reckon I can't fit in this cabinet, anymore? What am I gonna do? I really do like hearing what's going on—oh, no, here comes Momma.

"Emmybeth, what are you doing down there on the floor?" Momma asks as she sits down at the kitchen table. She still looks kind of pale and keeps rubbing her neck with a washrag. Man, I don't think I ever want babies if this is what you have to go through.

"I'm sorry, Momma. I, uh, was just looking for some peanut butter, and, uh, I knocked this can of beans out of the cabinet."

I spit out the first thing I can think of—never mind that she keeps the peanut butter in the top cabinet.

"Emmybeth, you know the peanut butter's not down in that cabinet. Besides, what are you doing in here? I thought you were reading in your room."

"Well, uh, I, uh . . ."

Oh, good. Why don't I say, uh, one more time?

"Emmybeth, could it be that you might have been trying to hide in the cabinet, and knocked the can of beans onto the floor?" Momma says as she looks straight into my eyes.

"Well, uh, uh, well . . . Momma?"

I look back at her as tears start brimming in my eyes. I bet I'm really gonna get in big trouble this time.

"Emmybeth, come on up here."

Momma holds out her arms, and I go sit in her lap as the tears start falling out of my eyes.

"Momma, I . . . I, uh, please don't be mad at me. I just like to hear what's going on with everybody. You hardly ever tell me anything, when I ask you about stuff. So, I, well, I just hide in the cabinet and . . ."

"Shush up, Emmybeth. I know."

"You know?" I can't believe my momma knows.

"Sure, I know, Emmybeth. Why do you think I was all the time trying to hush up Miss Hawkins and Grandma? I would try to change the subject when I thought it was getting out of hand. You know, I used to be like you when I was a little girl. I wanted to know what the grownups were talking about. I was curious, too; but, it's like I've told you before. You'll be grownup before you know it. You're already growing. You're too big to fit into that cabinet anymore, aren't you?"

I nod my head. Momma smiles and strokes my cheek.

"And," she continues, "You're almost getting too big for my lap. Shift around a little bit, Emmybeth." She laughs. "You're not going to fit in my lap much longer, but you'll always fit in my heart; you, Timmy, your daddy and our new baby, too. Everyone fits in my heart. Emmybeth, you're growing up so fast. You've got so many changes ahead of you the next few years. Just don't try to rush it too much. One day, you'll have all the worries you need. Don't try to take on the grownup stuff before you need to. There's plenty of time for that, later on—trust me."

Momma stands me up from her lap and looks straight into my eyes.

"You know what, Emmybeth? I think it's time you join our sewing circle, at least for a little while each week. You can help me serve the ladies their refreshments, then maybe Grandma can teach you some stitches, or maybe you can learn to do the appliqués from Mrs. Frazier. Either way, you can stay for the first few minutes, and then it's off to your room while we finish up. I know the other women won't mind as long as you don't overstay your welcome, and you mind me when I say it's time to scoot. All right?"

"Yes, Momma. I promise."

"Okay. There are a few things you need to understand, though, before the other ladies get here."

"What, Momma?" I say as I rub tears from my eyes.

"Well, Emmybeth, women need a place they can gather with other women to talk, laugh, and sometimes even cry together. It's important; but what's even more important is they need a place where they can just blow off steam and know that what they say will be kept in confidence by their friends. As important as it is to make the lap quilts for the old folks out at Sunny Meadows, or Christmas stockings, or whatever, it's equally important that these women come together, and have fellowship with each other. Sometimes we all say things we probably shouldn't, and sometimes we're just thinking out loud, just to figure things out. Does this make sense to you, Emmybeth?"

"Well, sorta, Momma. It's kinda like when Karen spends the night with me, and we talk about stuff just before we fall asleep," I say with a tiny smile, "Or just before you or daddy tell us 'enough is enough.'" Momma laughs at that.

"Just remember that, Emmybeth. The wisdom, the secrets, the pain and even the gossip you might hear from these women is yours to keep, Emmybeth. It's how we learn from each other. I couldn't have survived this past year without these women, Emmybeth. As much as I love your Daddy, and you and Timmy, these women gave me the strength I needed to make it through the year I've had."

"I think I understand, Momma," I say as I lay my head on her shoulder and breathe in her scent.

"Emmybeth, Darlene," Grandma exclaims as she comes through the back door. "What's goin' on with my girls this morning?"

"Oh, Grandma, it's just girl talk. You want to join us?" I say and look up at her with my best Grandma smile.

"That sounds mighty fine. I think some girl talk with my two best girls is more happiness than any grandma deserves!"

Grandma walks over and leans in for a hug. Me, Momma and Grandma squeeze each other real tight in a great big hug; with some love left over for our new baby. See, Jesus, sometimes I get everything just right.

And this time, I sure hope you're watching.

A Note from the Author

I hope you enjoyed reading *The Ivy Creek Sewing Circle*. If you would like to leave a review, please go to www.amazon.com or www.goodreads.com and do so today. I love hearing what readers have to say about the characters and stories I have so much fun creating.

If you would like to connect on social media, you can find me in the following places:

www.facebook.com/TammyRobinsonSmithauthor or www.instagram.com/trsauthor.

You can request personalized copies of my books at www.tammyrobinsonsmith.com, or you can send me a note via email at info@tammyrobinsonsmith.com. I would love to hear from you, so please feel free to reach out anytime.

Thank you for reading *The Ivy Creek Sewing Circle* and if you would like to learn more about my next novel, just turn the page!

Keep reading!

Didama's Garden Coming Soon!

When her baby daughter is ripped away from Didama, she believes she will never achieve true happiness in her lifetime.

Years later, she finds that happiness was just a few miles away and she never knew it. Come back to the Appalachian mountains with author Tammy Robinson Smith as she pens a heart-wrenching, but, inspirational tale of a mother's love that never dies.

Stories from the Heart of Appalachia

www.tammyrobinsonsmith.com

Made in the USA
Columbia, SC
13 September 2020